The Secrets of Cain's Castle

Case No. 3

A Belltown Mystery

By
T. M. Murphy

J. N. Townsend Publishing
Exeter, New Hampshire
2001

Printed in Canada
Published by J. N. Townsend Publishing
      4 Franklin Street
      Exeter, NH 03833
      603/778-9883
      800/333-9883
      www.jntownsendpublishing.com
      www.belltownmysteries.com

Library of Congress Cataloging-in-Publication Data
Murphy, Ted, 1969-
The secrets of Cain's castle / T.M. Murphy.
p. cm. –
 (A Belltown mystery ; Case #3)
Summary: Sixteen-year-old Orville Jacques takes a trip to Ireland
and becomes involved in a dangerous search for the lost treasure of
a fourteenth-century lord of the manor.
[1. Mystery and detective stories. 2. Ireland—Fiction. 3. Buried trea-
sure—Fiction. 4. Supernatural—Fiction.] I. Title.
PZ7.M9565 Sf 2001   2001041709
[Fic]—dc21
ISBN: 1-880158-38-8

Acknowledgments

I would like to thank the Kennedy, Corcoran, and Morris families for helping me discover my roots during my stay in Ireland. I would like to thank the Beevers, Matthews, Keating, and Kapulka families for their love and support. I would like to thank Joan Trainor, Jen Jensen, Kathy Sherwood, Kathy Rossow, Bill Atwood, Jeff Katz, Joe Wesolaski, Todd Oliveira, Sean and Brian Dailey for their loyalty.

A special thanks to U2, Danny Doyle, The Waterboys, Clannad, and Davy Spillane for being the Irish soundtrack for my youth. You are storytellers who teach me something new everyday!

For Colm Fitzgerald, Charlie McArdle, Finbar Philpott, Emmet Casserley, and everyone at the Dublin Garda Club: an ocean may divide us, but nothing will divide our friendship!

Dear Reader,

What you are about to read is a factual account of my trip to Ireland. There are events that seem unbelievable and have no logical explanation, or at least I haven't been able to find any. What haunts me most, especially during the midnight hours of my soul is the fact that I have no explanation . . .

       Orville Jacques

CHAPTER
ONE

I STILL COULDN'T believe it. I kept playing the scene over and over in my head, hoping there would be a different ending, but each time I heard the same stinging words, "My family is moving to Florida."

Maria Simpkins and I had finally stopped playing mind games and expressed our feelings for each other. We had been going out for three weeks and it was perfect. It was like we had been together forever. It seemed so right. Now, two weeks later, Maria had moved. Sure, we promised to call and write. Long-distance relationships almost never work out, especially when you're sixteen years old and live thousands of miles apart. Maria was gone out of my life, and I had to accept it.

I had spent the last week walking the halls of Belltown High in a trance, going from class to class as if someone else was controlling my movements. Without Maria in school, there wasn't much excitement in my life.

I went home. As I lay in my bed about to take a nap, all I had was a memory that I desperately tried to cling to. A week had passed, and I still thought of the last day. Walking along Cranberry Beach, Maria had picked up two identical smooth black stones and handed me one and put one into her pocket.

"Keep this with you, Orville, it will bring you luck."

"How do you know?" I asked.

"Just the fact that these stones are identical is a miracle to me. Therefore, they must be filled with miracles, so they will bring us luck."

"Where did you learn that?"

"I have my own theories about some things, and I also know that if you hold onto that stone, you'll think of me. Just like I'll think of you." She turned her head away from me for a second before she continued. "But, there will be a time when we'll both have to throw our stones back to the sea, so they will give other people miracles and memories."

I could see the tears in her eyes, and I wanted to make the moment more bearable. "Maria, you're depressing me."

"I'm sorry, Orville." Maria smiled and I focused on that smile, knowing that I might not see it again.

The knock on my bedroom door brought me back to reality. I could play that scene over and over again, but the truth was Maria was gone. I returned the black stone to my pocket while getting up from my bed.

"Who is it?" I managed between yawns.

"Dad wants to talk to you," said my little sister, Jackie.

"OK, I'll be right down."

"Orville, he wants to talk to you in the *living room*." Jackie emphasized living room, even though she didn't have to. She knew it and I knew it. Whenever we got into trouble and Dad or Mom wanted to talk to us, it always seemed to be the living room—never the family room. I don't think it was conscious on their part. It just always seemed to happen that way. Living room meant trouble—family room meant good news. I was trying to think of what I had done to get an invitation to the living room. Other than algebra, for which I was destined to go to summer school, my grades were decent. I couldn't think of anything, so I decided to stop thinking about it and just go and face it.

I walked into the living room and saw my dad holding a piece of paper in his hands and my mom sitting beside him on the couch. Both of them, I thought, twice the trouble. I knew dad wasn't holding my report card because that didn't come out till after Christmas break.

Dad looked up and said, "Orville, take a seat."

"What's wrong, Dad?"

"Nothing's wrong. Why is it every time I ask to talk to one of you kids in here you assume the worst? Mom and I wanted to talk to you in private because we want to tell you something." Dad took off his reading glasses and folded them.

"Oh, OK, what's that?" I finally sat down.

"Remember I applied to teach in Belltown, Ireland, as part of that sister-town-school exchange program?"

"Sister town?" I had no idea what he was talking about.

"Yes, Belltown, Ireland, is the sister town of Belltown, Cape Cod. Only one teacher was going to be chosen from our town to teach for two months and vice versa."

Dad tried jogging my memory, but I really couldn't remember, but I said, "Oh, yeah, now I remember." He must have mentioned it during the Katherine Stinson murder case, I thought.

"Well, I got this letter two weeks ago." He handed me the letter and I scanned it briefly.

"Wow, that's great, they accepted you! I'm really happy for you, Dad."

"The school sent me two free round-trip airline tickets."

"Yeah." I was beginning to wonder why this wasn't a family meeting. After all, Dad would be away for two months. He turned to Mom and she said, "I was going to go with your father for your two weeks of Christmas break, and have you kids stay with your grandmother but I decided not to."

"Why?" I asked.

"Well, this is my first year of running the tutoring center, and during holiday break I'm going to be tutoring a lot of kids, getting them ready for their SATs. So, we're thinking . . ." Mom stopped for a second. "Orville, we know you've been a little upset lately with Will's death in November and now Maria's moving, and we thought a couple of weeks in Ireland would be a nice change of scenery."

"You're saying I should go to Ireland?"

"If you want to." Dad jumped in. "It's your choice."

"What would I do? I mean, you'd be teaching all day, wouldn't you?"

"Yes, they don't have much of a Christmas break. I start teaching our third day there. But, I wouldn't want you living by my schedule. Both your mother's parents were Irish and my mother is Irish."

So?" I didn't understand.

"We were thinking of giving you the addresses of all your relatives, and you could bounce around Ireland doing your own thing."

"You mean backpacking?" I asked surprised, thinking of the freedom I would be allowed.

"Yes, you're sixteen and considering what you've been through this past year with all that crime solving, I think you can handle the responsibility of traveling."

"How long would I go for?" I started to get excited.

"Your break is two weeks and all your teachers agreed that you could miss another week, providing you make it up when you come home. The only one who gave us a hard time was your algebra teacher, Mr. Reasons, but we all know where you're headed with that."

"Summer school," I grunted.

"Yes, I know, but let's not think of that right now." Mom always tried to make me feel better about my inability to find the meaning of X.

"Exactly, you're a chip off the old block." Dad smiled.

"Blockhead is more like it." We all laughed at mom's joke. "So, do you want to go?" They both asked.

"Of course, I do," I shouted.

"Wait," Dad interrupted, "There are a few conditions. The first two days I want you to be with me at Belltown, so we can have some time together."

"Yeah, no problem. Where is Belltown?"

"It's twenty miles south of Dublin." He answered my question quickly and continued on with the conditions. "No hitchhiking. I always want you to take public transportation. No traveling after dark. You have to keep in contact with me. Call me when you are going to a different relative's house and when you get there. Also, your English teacher wants you to write a five-page paper on your experience."

"That's Mrs. Holcomb for you. I probably shouldn't ask this question, but why are you letting me miss school?"

"It's only a week of school for one thing, and in that time you'll probably learn more about your Irish heritage then you'll ever read in a book. Someday, hopefully, you'll go to France and learn about the Jacques family," Dad said.

"Boring." Mom laughed and I joined in.

"Oh, and there is one other condition." Dad paused. "There better be no searching for mysteries over there in the land of myths. Got it?"

"Got it." I smiled.

"Good, because you've given your mother and me heart problems this past year playing the young Sherlock

The Secrets of Cain's Castle

Holmes." Dad frowned.

"It's not my fault that I've stumbled into those mysteries," I argued.

They both stared at me.

"No more mysteries for Orville Jacques," I stated confidently.

"Are you sure?" Mom asked.

"Positively." I fully believed my answer.

A pounding rain greeted me as I got off the bus at Connolly Station in Dublin. I didn't care about the rain. It could rain buckets for all I cared. The point was I was finally on my own. Don't get me wrong, spending the first two days with my dad in Belltown, Ireland, was fun, but I was itching to travel and see all of Ireland.

I could tell Dad was just as excited to begin teaching in a foreign country as I was to begin my adventure. I knew Mom was right, traveling would get my mind off Maria and Will. At least, I was hoping she was right, but that didn't stop me from clutching the black stone that I kept in my raincoat pocket. I walked briskly through the rain and over to the line of taxis that waited for soaked passengers.

"You need a ride, lad?" the middle-aged driver smiled as he opened the door for me before I could answer.

"Yes, I guess so," I said as he ushered me into the front seat and grabbed my backpack and put it into the trunk.

"So, now, where would ya be heading on this day?"

He turned to me and his smile was infectious.

I smiled back, "Sheriff's Street, sir."

His eyes widened and the smile vanished.

"My name is Joe, lad. Joe Ivory." He put his hand out and I shook it.

"Orville. Orville Jacques."

"Well, Orville, you wouldn't want to be going to Sheriff's Street. They're a bad lot who hang out on Sheriff's Street. You'll lose your wallet before you can blink your eyes," Joe said while putting on his directional signal and pulling out.

"I'll be OK, Joe. After all, I'm going to visit a policeman."

"A Garda. I know them all. What's your man's name?"

"Colm O'Connell."

"Colm, you're surely teasing me. Colm O'Connell and I are old chums. Is he a relative, lad?"

"No, Joe. He's the cousin of a friend of mine, Shane O'Connell."

"The detective," Joe answered matter-of-factly.

"How did you know that?" I was in shock.

"I met Shane when he traveled over here years ago with a couple of other lads. I see you have your backpack, so why are you traveling Ireland, Mr. Orville Jacques? Surely, you're not Irish."

"My dad's father was French, but his mother is Irish. And both my mom's parents were Irish. So, I might have a French name, but I'm more Irish than you may think."

"Aye, that you are. You're French and Irish, I guess." Joe paused, "That would make you a French fry." He let out a roar. And I joined him as he almost hit a parked delivery truck. He turned the steering wheel just in time, and I looked over at him and we let out more laughter. After about half a minute, we calmed down and Joe began asking me more questions. He was particularly interested in my travels, giving me advice on different places to see.

"Now, Orville, what do you want to be when you get older?" Joe changed subjects as quickly as he changed lanes.

"I don't know." I looked at him blankly.

"You have no idea?"

"Well, no. I'm only sixteen," I said defensively.

"Easy, lad. Don't get all worked up. You shouldn't know where you're going in your future."

" Why?" I asked, even though I agreed.

"Because you don't know where you've been." He nodded his head as we pulled up to the curb on Sheriff's Street, "That's why you're on this trip. To see where you've been."

He opened the door and grabbed my backpack as I said the words softly to myself. "You don't know where you're going if you don't know where you've been."

I reached into my pocket and pulled out the colorful bills in full view and looked for a ten-pound note.

"Orville, put your money away. You won't last long in this neighborhood if you're that casual," Joe said while shoving my hands back into my pockets.

"Oh, sorry, Joe. What do I owe you?" I whispered.

"Not a dime from a friend of the O'Connells."

"But, your boss?" I argued.

"Are you mad, man? I'm me own boss. But, I will not stay any longer on this street. I shouldn't leave you here, but Colm should be walking down the street in a matter of minutes. So, I will be off, and if anyone messes with you just say you're friends with Colm O'Connell and Joe Ivory."

"Thank you, Joe." I shook his hand.

"Don't give it a care and good luck on your journey." Joe jumped into his cab and zoomed off.

I realized I was standing in the rain. My attitude before arriving on Sheriff's Street was: Hey, I'm American. I've been to some of the toughest parts of Boston. I've faced all sorts of danger in my young life, so what's so bad about Sheriff's Street? I saw a group of four teenagers checking me out. They looked between sixteen and eighteen years old except for one. He looked like he was only twelve. They all looked alike, and I wondered if maybe they were brothers. The tallest in the group motioned to the other three and they formed a huddle and occasionally looked my way and laughed. I didn't need an interpreter to figure out what they were talking about—ME. The voice from the tallest kid interrupted my thoughts.

"Hey, you're a Yank are ya not?" He smiled a fake smile. I also noticed that he was wearing a black eye patch over his right eye.

"Yes, I'm from America." I knew I couldn't show my fear.

The huddle broke up and they all walked slowly toward me.

"Well, well, well. We should feel so honored to have a Yank walk our slums. Don't ya think so, Liam?" The kid with the eye patch turned to his friend, but kept his one eye on me. I could see a faint smile appear when he spotted the watch on my wrist.

"Indeed, I am honored." Liam bowed to me and the group laughed, and I realized they had surrounded me. My pulse quickened. Where is Colm O'Connell, I thought as the kid with the eye patch moved closer.

"What brings you to Sheriff's Street, mate?" He was now about ten feet away.

"I'm … I'm on vacation and I came to see my friend Colm O'Connell." I thought that might scare them, but it had the opposite effect. The kid with the eye patch laughed and the rest followed his lead.

"So, you're on holiday. Not only is he a Yank. He's a rich Yank, fellas."

"No, really I'm not." My objections fell on deaf ears.

"Well, you're going to need that bumbling O'Connell."

He walked over and grabbed my hand.

"What are you doing?" I tried to break loose, but Liam and another kid grabbed my arms.

"A rich Yank like you won't miss this." The kid with the eye patch ripped my watch off my wrist and admired it for a minute as I tried to break free of the hold.

"Patch, try it on," said Liam.

"Your name is Patch." I tried to say it calmly. I knew there was no sense fighting the hold Liam and the other kid had on me.

"Fitting name. Don't ya think?" He pointed to his eye patch.

"Yes. Well, Patch, could you please give me back my watch. It means a lot to me."

Patch laughed and ignored my plea while looking at the back of my watch. "Mates, listen to this: 'To Will, Love Katherine.' How *sweet*. Is Katherine your lass?" he asked as he put the watch on his wrist.

"No. My grandfather gave it to me. It was his watch."

There was no use explaining that Will wasn't my grandfather, but he was like one to me. There was no compassion in that one eye. It was just filled with hate, and I think Patch was more psyched knowing he was taking something that meant more than material value to me. I couldn't hold back my anger anymore.

"Give it back!" I shouted.

"I'll give you something, mate." Patch cocked his arm back and was about to punch me when a yell from up the street interrupted us.

"I got it. I got it, mates." A kid ran up the street holding a cage with an animal in it. They all turned their attention from me to their friend with the cage.

"We'll be driving in grand style tonight." The kid with the cage continued and they all laughed. Liam and his friend let go of me and ran over to the kid with the cage.

"Let's get a sports car." Liam joined in.

I had no idea what they were talking about, but frankly I didn't care. I knew this was my chance to make a run for it. I thought briefly about charging at Patch and trying to grab my watch, but I knew there would be no chance for an escape if I did that. It seemed like they totally forgot about me and I wasn't about to remind them. I slithered down a puddle-filled alley and then bolted. I heard distant yells of "There goes the Yank!" and "Get the Yank!" After I ran for a minute I looked behind me and saw there was no one in sight. I knew if they were chasing me, they would have easily caught up, considering I was lugging my forty-pound backpack. I figured they probably yelled so they could watch me run like a crazy man and have a good laugh.

I spent the next half hour cautiously walking the streets, trying desperately to find Colm O'Connell before Patch and his gang found me. My prayers went unanswered as I turned a corner and saw Patch and his gang at the end of the street, hiding behind a building by a stop sign. Fortunately, I spotted them before they spotted me. I ducked around the corner and spied on them. Were they hiding there thinking I would be coming back that way? I wondered. There were so many street corners, why would they pick that one? Why wouldn't they split up and look for me? All my questions were answered when a red car came to a halt at the stop sign. Liam sprinted over and opened the passenger door of the car. The kid who had been holding the cage ran over and opened the cage and let the animal out in the car. The woman driver screamed and leaped out of the car, ranting all the way up the street.

"C'mon mates," Liam yelled, letting them know the coast was clear.

Patch and the others ran to the car and were about to jump in when two police officers came out of no-where and began chasing them. They all scattered, go-ing in different directions except for Liam and the young-est boy. They were heading my way, followed by a po-liceman who was quickly being outpaced by their youth. I could tell it wouldn't be long before they got away. Liam was laughing and pointing at the policeman as he was easily outdistancing him. Maybe that's why Liam didn't see me put my foot out as he turned the corner. He had been going so fast that his face kissed the pave-ment. The laughing quickly became sobs of pain. The policeman grabbed the young boy who had stopped to see if Liam was all right. Liam lay on the ground moan-ing.

"Good work, lad." The policeman smiled over at me.

"No problem." I shrugged.

"Could you hold onto this one for a second while I cuff the other one?" He handed me the young boy who was shaking with fright. The policeman picked Liam up with one hand and looked at his bloody face.

"I believe that under all that blood is Mr. Liam McCormick. Am I right?"

Liam didn't say anything, he just glared at me.

"Surely, you know what this means, Liam. You're on probation and you just broke it, scaring that poor woman. I believe you'll do at least six months."

"I didn't do anything." Liam grunted.

The other officer approached, wiping his brow. "Good work, Finbar. The other snipes got away."

"I really can't take the credit, sir. This lad tripped Mr. McCormick, and I was able to catch up."

"You don't say." The policeman looked over at me.

"Thanks, lad." He paused. "But what are you doing here?"

"I'm looking for Colm O'Connell," I said.

The man brightened up. "Don't cast your eyes any further." He put his hand out, "You must be Orville Jacques, Shane's friend."

"Yes, I am." I smiled, knowing I was finally safe.

"Orville Jacques, I'll remember that," Liam said.

"I heard that, Mr. McCormick. Finbar, could you please see that Mr. McCormick gets to his cell quickly, so he won't miss teatime."

"Sure sir, but what about little Davey Evans?" He looked over to the young boy who was still shaking.

"I'll take care of Davey myself." He nodded. "If you will excuse me, Orville. I have to talk to the little one for a second."

I stood there feeling relieved that I had found Colm, but I was still upset my watch was gone. Whenever I wore that watch I felt Will was with me, and now some lowlife was wearing it. A small rock landed right in front of me and brought me out of my trance. I turned around and looked up and saw Patch standing on the roof of a run-down tenement. He was pointing at my watch on his wrist and laughing. Then he made a gun with his fingers, pointed, pulled the trigger, and blew the imaginary smoke away. Before I could turn to Colm, Patch jumped from rooftop to rooftop and soon was swallowed by the gray day.

"Davey's a good lad. He just looks up to the wrong types."

Colm interrupted my gaze.

"Oh, yes. Well, what did you tell him?" I asked.

"I gave him a warning and told him if you lie down with dogs you'll rise up with fleas. I just hope he heeds my advice. Now let's get you by a warm peat fire before the damp gets into your bones." Colm smiled.

"Yes, that would be nice," I said, giving one last look up at the tenement building. My parents had told me to stay out of adventures, but when it came to Patch, I knew I might not have a choice. In my damp bones, I felt our paths would cross again . . .

CHAPTER
TWO

W<small>HILE WE SAT</small> by the peat fire sipping tea in Colm's flat, I told him about my encounter with Patch. After I finished telling him the significance of the watch, Colm shook his head, rose and poured me another cup of tea.

"Orville, I will use all my power to catch Patch McCormick and get your watch back. But, I will not lie to you, he is a slippery one." Colm sighed.

"McCormick. Isn't that Liam's last name?"

"Indeed, they are brothers. I do feel sorry for the poor lads. They are orphans and all they have is each other." Colm paused, "But my sympathy ends when they break the law and that's an everyday occurrence."

"What happened to their parents?"

"Who knows? They just left the two lads to fend for themselves. So they began stealing, but Liam has been the only one who ever gets caught. I'll tell you one thing, Patch will be angry when he finds out his brother is finally going to do time. And since he knows that you helped catch Liam, it might be wise if you left Dublin and began your journey." Colm tossed a brick of peat on the fire.

"No way. I intend to spend at least three days in Dublin before I hit the countryside." Patch wasn't going to ruin my trip.

"Shane told me you were determined." Colm gave in with a laugh. "Orville, just promise me that you won't tour Sheriff's Street again."

"I won't."

"Good, now you better ring your dad and tell him about today's adventure."

"You mean how I got off the bus, met you, and spent a lazy day drinking tea by the fire." I winked.

Colm laughed, "Yes, a lazy day."

We both knew if I told my dad about my first day's adventure, it would be my last day's adventure!

Colm took the day off and showed me around the city, but not before he put out an all-points bulletin for the arrest of Patch McCormick. I didn't object to him taking the day off because I could tell that he was concerned about showing me the finer parts of Dublin so my first day wouldn't taint my vision of the city. We went to the National Gallery, and looked at sculptures and works by Ireland's great artists. When we came out of the gallery, it was like Colm heard my stomach screaming for lunch.

"Are you a steak man, Orville?" he asked squinting.

"I love a good steak." I was relieved we were on the same wavelength.

"Good, I know a nice place off Grafton Street that will have it on your plate in ten minutes."

"Awesome!" I said and jumped into his car without realizing what I was doing. I didn't understand why Colm was laughing until I saw the steering wheel in front of me. I was so hungry that I had forgotten where I was. Irish cars have the driver's side on the right side of the car. I opened the door and slowly got out.

"Now would ya be wanting the keys, driver?" Colm tried to contain his laughter but just couldn't help it.

"Very funny." I gave him a plain face before I joined in.

I forgot all about my hunger when I saw her standing with a group of shabbily dressed people outside the restaurant. I guessed she was about sixteen or seventeen. Our eyes met and locked for a minute. She wore a tattered dress. Her long brown hair seemed to be fighting the wind as she clutched her shawl around her neck. I looked at the people she was standing with, wondered if they were all homeless as our eyes locked again. She had deep green eyes, a color I had never seen before. There was another thing about her that was different from the rest—she wasn't smiling. Everyone else in the group seemed to be laughing at a joke, but she was just staring at me, and I was staring back at her.

It seemed we both realized our staring at the same time and turned away. Colm tipped his tweed cap at the group and then opened the door for me. The restaurant was nothing I had expected or I had seen before. Every inch of it was decorated with old movie posters and director's chairs at the tables. "What's the deal with this place?" I asked Colm as I sat down.

"The owner is an old movie buff," Colm answered.

"I guess so. What's this place called?" I asked, interested.

"The Blue Parrot. It's named after a club from a Humphrey Bogart movie called '*Casablanca*,'" Colm answered while waving to a waiter.

"Really, I gotta tell my dad. He loves old movies, and I know that's one of his favorites."

The waiter came over and we ordered our steaks. As we waited I kept thinking about the girl with the green eyes. Something about her intrigued me. Ten minutes later, we were eating our steaks, but I couldn't hold in my curiosity anymore.

"Colm, those people who are hanging outside, are they homeless?" I asked the question feeling guilty as I took another bite of the tender steak.

"It depends on how you look at it," he said, wiping his mouth with his napkin.

"What do you mean?" I didn't understand.

"Those people outside are called Travelers. You see, some people might think they're homeless, but I don't think the Travelers think they are. You know the saying,

'Home is where your heart is?'" Colm looked up from his plate.

"Yes."

"Well, most of the Travelers feel all of Ireland is in their heart and that's what they do. They travel to be at home with themselves. Am I making any sense?"

"Perfect sense, it just sounds like a different lifestyle."

"That's what I like about you, Orville Jacques. You don't judge people. I've told other Americans about the Travelers' lifestyle, and they thought they were crazy. In fact, a lot of Irish think the Travelers are crazy. Don't get me wrong, there are some bad ones. I won't tolerate that. But, what gets me angry is the stereotyping that goes on; Travelers are all bad people. I don't like stereotyping, Orville. It's dangerous."

Suddenly, the Traveler girl ran into the restaurant and pounded her fist on the bar. Her face was flushed with fear. "Water! I need water!" she screamed.

"Get outta here," the barkeep snarled.

"Please, I need water for me da!"

I sensed trouble, so I got up and went over to the girl.

The barkeep pounded his fist down on the counter, "I said get out of here before I get the Garda."

"But me da, me da is choking! I need water."

I didn't even pause. I knew what I had to do. I bumped into the girl as I ran past her and out the door. I saw the group of Travelers around an old man who had a long white beard. The white in his beard made his purple face look even darker. The man was wheezing, grasping his throat.

"Move!" I forced my way through the circle and got behind the man, put my arms around him the way I was taught, and began to thrust upward. Suddenly, I felt a sharp pain in my back. Someone was punching me on the back and I recognized the voice, "What are ye doin' to me da? You're killing me da!"

I turned my head and yelled at her, "Back off, I'm trying to save him."

The girl backed off, and a few seconds later a piece of food flew out of the man's mouth and he began coughing as he lowered himself to the pavement.

"Sir, are you OK?" I crouched down.

"Yes, lad," He said slowly.

The group around him cheered, and Colm came over and patted me on the back. The girl rushed over and helped the man up.

"What was that thing you did to me, lad?"

"The Heimlich maneuver," Colm answered for me.

"Well, whatever ye call it, I'm much obliged." The man smiled.

"Don't thank me. Thank my health issues teacher, Mr. Chicoine." I laughed thinking of Mr. Chicoine's words, "Someday, you'll be grateful you learned this."

"What's yer name, lad?" He put his hand out.

"Orville." I shook it.

"My name is Feargal." His eyes twinkled.

"Come on, Da. We have to be on our way."

"Well, thanks again, lad."

"No problem."

The girl and the man walked up two streets and then were gone.

"Orville, you've had quite a couple of days. You're a hero." Colm smiled and I blushed out of embarrassment.

"For saving a Traveler, he's no hero," the barkeep growled from the doorway of The Blue Parrot.

Colm whispered, "Excuse me for a second." He turned and glared. "Sir, Colm O'Connell, Dublin Garda. I would like to have a little chat with you about your service to customers."

I could see the arrogance in the barkeep's face vanish. As I turned to go back into the restaurant, I saw something lying on the ground. I knew exactly what it was—her shawl.

I stared at the embroidery—C-é-i-l-í. I had no idea how to pronounce the word so I grabbed the first person passing.

"Excuse me, sir, but how do you say this word?" I pointed at it.

The man continued walking while looking down at the word. "Kayleigh, lad."

"Kayleigh."

"Beautiful name, isn't it?" He smiled and was on his way.

"Yes, it is," I said to myself and folded the shawl as light rain began to fall.

After Colm gave the barkeep a good scare for being rude to the Traveler girl, we finished our steaks and went back to his flat. I found out Colm didn't exactly have the day off. He switched shifts and had to work the early night shift, which was from 4:00 PM to 12:00 AM. Before he left I asked him where he thought those Travelers kept camp. He told me that they camped in the outskirts of Dublin.

"What stop would you get off if you took a bus?" I asked nonchalantly.

"Oh, I would say you'd get off at Crooked Path, and their camp is about a five-minute walk down the path." Colm stopped. "Wait, just a minute here, you're not thinking of checking out their camp, are you? Because there are some bad ones too, and you could get mugged!"

"No. I was just wondering how they got back to their camp." I bit the side of my mouth.

"Oh." Colm smiled in relief. "Not many take buses, they usually have horse carts or they just walk it. Well, I better be off. What will you be doing?" he asked as he put on his Garda jacket.

"I'm going to walk down Grafton Street and look for some gifts for my brother and sister." I grabbed my daypack and headed out the door with Colm.

"Sounds grand, I'll see you when the rooster crows."

"Or maybe a little later." I laughed.

Grafton Street was about a ten-minute walk from Colm's flat on Adalaide Road. There was a soft rain falling, but I was getting to the point where I almost expected rain. It really didn't bother me, and I stopped for a minute and listened to a couple of street musicians playing guitars and harmonicas and singing The

Waterboys' "Fisherman's Blues." I hummed along thinking of how many times I had heard the Irish band's song on WMVY , thousands of miles away, and liked it, but the smiles on the street musicians' faces as I threw a pound into their guitar cases gave me a new appreciation for the song.

I hummed away as I continued down the street. Almost everything on the street was suited for tourists— "Kiss me, I'm Irish" sweatshirts, stuffed leprechaun dolls, green mugs, and so on. Maybe, it's because I come from a tourist haven, Cape Cod, that I didn't want to buy my family those kinds of gifts. I wanted to give each of them something *really* Irish, so I figured my best bet was to go down side streets. Approaching one side street, a man shouted to me from an alleyway. I was hesitant to go over, but I could see he had a small table set up.

"Lad, come here and take a look. I bet you'll find something nice for your lass." My heart sank for a moment thinking of Maria.

"I don't have a lass." I said.

"That's OK, you have your whole life to find one." He chuckled and his two chins almost hit the table.

"You must have a mum." He pointed at some fake green jewelry.

"No, thanks. I don't think so." I began to walk away.

"You need a cap. How 'bout this? Five pounds and you'll be the envy of your mates." He showed me an ugly neon-green tweed cap.

"No, thanks." I shook my head, trying not to laugh while thinking of the reaction I would get from the gang at Belltown High when I walked in with that. Envy was not the word.

"You win, lad, and I lose. Good day to you. "The man sat down and pulled out a knife and a wooden figure of something and began carving.

"Is that a donkey you're carving?" I asked.

"Yes, it is. I'm just finishing it." He looked up almost surprised that I was still there.

"May I take a look?"

"Sure." He handed it to me.

I don't know anything about woodcarving, but I knew enough to realize the man had talent. "My sister, Jackie, likes animals. I know she'd love something like this. How much?" I pulled out my wallet.

"I never sell my carvings. I do them to pass the time."

"You should sell them. Not everybody likes that tourist stuff. Sir, you have a talent and you should be using it."

"Ah, thanks, lad." He blushed. I could see he wasn't used to praise.

"What's your sister's name again?" He picked up his knife and I handed him the donkey.

"Jackie."

"And yours?" He turned the donkey over, and the knife moved like lightning.

"Orville."

"Orville, good to meet you. My name is Seamus Flanagan." He didn't look up as he worked the knife while the shavings fell to the ground.

"Do you sell things on the street for a living?"

"I'm also a painter." I watched the inscription appear: To sister Jackie—Love, your brother, Orville.

"Oh, you're an artist."

"No, a house painter." He laughed, "Actually, I paint anything—stables, pubs, I even painted a castle a couple of weeks ago."

"A castle," I said, surprised.

"Well, a few rooms in the castle." He looked up and handed me the donkey, "Here you go, Orville."

I was about to ask him how much I owed him when a man pedaled his bike down the alleyway, interrupting our negotiations.

"Seamus Flanagan, I'm surprised to see you're among the living." The man laughed as he rang his bike bell.

"If you excuse me one minute, Orville." Seamus walked over to the man. "Keep it down, Johnny."

The man didn't acknowledge his request. "Ye were a sight for sore eyes last night. The liquor controlled your tongue. All that talk about the lost Mac Farlane map. "The man howled with laughter, but laughter didn't enter Seamus's eyes. His eyes were like round pebbles and his red face turned ghost white.

"You're talking mad, man!" Seamus yelled. "I said no such thing."

"No, Seamus, you're the one who was talking mad. Telling the pub that you'll be rich enough to stop working. You were in a bad way." The man pedaled down the alley ringing his bike bell, "Sorry, Seamus, that must hurt your head." He laughed and was quickly out of sight. Only the echo of his bell remained.

Seamus had a faraway look. I think he forgot I was even there. He was packing up his things, mumbling. I finally interrupted, "Seamus, how much do I owe you?"

He broke out of his trance and smiled, but it didn't seem genuine. It seemed forced. "Nothing, lad." He continued his packing.

"I have to pay you something," I argued.

He stopped for a second and thought, "Ye can't put a price tag on creativity." He turned his back and went into his bag.

"I wouldn't feel right if I didn't pay you," I insisted.

I think Seamus was annoyed at my persistence, "I'm not going to charge ye money. The joy you gave me knowing you liked my work was enough. Now, I gotta get going, but let me wrap the donkey for ye, so it doesn't get wet." He grabbed an old light-colored cloth that was in his bag and put the donkey in it and wrapped it up. "Now where are ye staying Orville?" He asked.

"Adalaide Road for a day or two more with Colm O'Connell."

"Yes, Mr. O'Connell, I know him. Very well respected." He was saying the words, but I don't think his mind was in the conversation. The man on the bike had really upset him, and I had to settle my own curiosity.

"What that man said upset you. Why?"

Seamus's eyes narrowed and he paused for a minute "Orville, everyone has their own problems. Some people can overcome them. I can't. Mine live in the bottle."

"You mean you drink a lot?" I didn't know how else

to ask the question.

"Yes, I'm a drunk or an alcoholic or whatever ye want to call it." He paused and then gave a sad, slow laugh "Don't ever start drinking, Orville, the stuff will surely kill ye. Surely, it will . . ."

The bus driver shook his head in disbelief but agreed to drop me off at Crooked Path when he came to that stop. It was going to take twenty minutes until the bus got there and that validated my decision to shop a little while before I jumped on the bus. After all, if it took twenty minutes by bus, it would take Céilí and her dad a couple of hours to walk that distance. I don't know why I was so determined to make sure she got her shawl back. Maybe I just didn't want her to think that I thought of her like the barkeep and other people did? Maybe the fact that I was going out of my way to return her shawl meant that I did think that way and was avoiding those thoughts? I don't know. I was confused. But then I thought maybe I was just plain intrigued by her way of life and wanted to find out more. As I looked at the beautiful multicolored shawl I had a feeling that it meant more than comfort to Céilí like what my watch meant to me. I had nothing to back up this belief; just a strange way of knowing that was the real reason I had to return the shawl to her.

I could see the bus driver's raised brow in his mirror as he pulled the handle and opened the door. "Crooked Path," he yelled. I hesitated for a second then got up out of my seat, went down the aisle, and heard some whispers behind me.

"Thanks," I said to the bus driver.

"Now remember, lad, a bus comes by here every half hour but ye have to wave it down." His look said it all, "Do you really want to do this?"

"Yes, thanks again."

"Lad, do ye know what you're headed for?" A burly-looking farmer questioned me as I was about to get off the bus.

"Yes, Sir," I said politely, hoping to take the edge off his voice. It didn't.

"Do ya know why they call it 'Crooked Path'? Don't think it's because the path is crooked. It's crooked all right. It got its name from the people who hide in the path, waiting to snatch whatever trinkets you got." The man pointed at my backpack.

My commonsense told me to listen to the man, but my gut said to get off the bus.

The bus driver, whose patience had run out, asked, "Well, what will it be, on or off?"

"Off. But thanks for the warning." I tried to force a smile at the farmer and the bus driver, but they both grunted in unison, "Crazy Yank."

The door shut behind me and the bus roared off down the narrow road. I took a deep breath when I spotted the rotting wooden sign that was painted in white lettering: Crooked Path. Underneath the lettering was an arrow pointing to a trail going uphill. I felt my heart suddenly jump a beat as I began to follow the trail. What am I? Crazy, I thought, looking at the trail that zigzagged throughout low-lying brush.

The rain was steady, and I could tell nightfall was around the corner. What I was most concerned about was what else was around the corner as I slowly made my way uphill. I reached into my pocket and clutched my stone. As crazy as it probably was, something told me to continue and I would be safe. Finally, after about fifteen minutes, I came to the top of the trail, a small hill above a meadow. I thought I heard rustling behind me, so my natural instinct was to hit the dirt. I went down on all fours and looked behind me, but it was now too dark to see anything. I was hoping I had just imagined the noise, but due to my past experiences, I didn't want to take any chances, so I listened intently. I didn't hear anything and that almost made me more nervous. If I could hear the rustling again I could make a run for it or figure out the cause of it like maybe birds or something, but since I couldn't hear anything I was paralyzed. Distant music and voices from the meadow brought me out of my paralysis and took my attention from what was behind me to what was in front of me. It was the Travelers' camp. A huge bonfire lit the camp and made it easy for me to spy as I stayed down on all fours.

The camp consisted of seven or eight painted wagons. There were also a couple of cars without any tires on blocks and a couple of modern RVs. It seemed as though there were almost two camps: one, the painted wagons, and the other, the modern campers. The painted wagons were in a semicircle around the fire. There was a man stirring a smoking iron pot while another man, whose back was to me, gestured wildly to a group of listeners. He turned his head for a brief second, and the fire illuminated his face. It was the man I had saved from choking. It was Feargal. A wave of relief flowed through my body as I began to get up from the ground. I knew I would be safe once Feargal saw me. But, suddenly, out of nowhere, that sense of relief vanished as I felt an arm wrap around my throat. I shook my head in a wild frenzy, struggling to break free.

"Don't move or else," the voice whispered.

I knew the tone in the voice. I had heard that tone before. It wasn't a threat. It was a promise . . .

CHAPTER THREE

I KNEW I shouldn't breathe because one false move and it would be the end.

I was trembling uncontrollably, wanting to make a move, but at the same time waiting for the knife to strike. It didn't. There was no movement of any kind. It was like he was thinking of what to do next. I knew this was my time to act. In one quick action, I raised my hands and grabbed the arm that was around my throat and bit him. Yes, bit him! I knew he wasn't expecting that as he let out a cry of pain and lost the grip he had on me. I was free but not for long. He recovered quickly, and he jumped on top of me and knocked me to the ground. We rolled wildly in the bush, struggling to get leverage on each other. My animal instincts took over as I punched, kicked, and scratched him. I felt the man's long hair in the dark and pulled it. We both let out grunts as we rolled through the bush, tumbling out of control down the hill. I felt my glasses fly off as the force of the roll made us break free from each other and roll our separate ways until we came to a stop at the Travelers' camp. Since I didn't have my glasses, everything was blurry as I squinted to focus on the camp and look for Feargal. But, I didn't have time to focus as two bodies jumped on me and held me down. I couldn't make out their faces as another person blinded me even more while waving a torch a foot away from my face.

"Aye, ye think ye can come to Crooked Path and make all your riches off the Travelers. Well, you got another thing comin'. "

The male's voice was fierce as he waved the torch closer to my face, and I thought my face was going to catch fire.

"Please stop! I know Feargal! I know Feargal!" I screamed at the top of my lungs.

"What?" the man asked, astonished, abruptly pulling the torch back a little.

"I know Feargal! I came to see Feargal and Céilí!"

The man didn't even pause. "Feargal, come quick!"

"Just a minute. I'm taking care of . . ." Feargal yelled in the background, but was interrupted by the torch holder.

"Feargal, now!"

A couple of seconds passed while the two other people kept their hold on me.

"Feargal, this Yank crook says he knows you." The

voice sounded skeptical as he waved the torch in front of my face again.

"Oh, me goodness, man. That's the lad I was just telling ye about. He's the lad who saved me. Take that torch from his face," Feargal demanded, and I gasped gratefully.

The man paused for a minute, surprised about the turn around in events, and the other two reluctantly let go as Feargal helped me up off the ground.

"Now what is goin' on, lad?" Feargal asked in an even tone.

"Well, I came to see you and I heard a noise, so I hid in the bushes and was jumped by some guy," I said quickly and out of breath. Feargal didn't say anything.

"The guy. Y'know the guy who gave me this." I pointed to my nose and the blood flowing freely.

"There was no man in those bushes, lad."

"What do you mean? You must have seen us rolling down the hill," I said, frustrated, and even more because I didn't have my glasses to see his reaction.

"I saw you, but I didn't know it was you. I did pick these up." He handed me my glasses and I put them on.

"If you saw me and you found my glasses and you see my bloody nose, not to mention a black eye I feel forming, how can you say there was no man? Why would I roll down a hill by myself?" The group began laughing and it angered and confused me even more.

Feargal then cleared up my confusion, "Because, lad, does *she* look like a man?" He pointed over to where he had come from, and staring at me with eyes blazing like the bonfire behind her was Céilí.

"What!" I gasped, and they all laughed at my obvious embarrassment except for Céilí, who was fuming.

"Why were ye hiding in those bushes!" She stormed up to me.

"I was ... ah ... comin' ... to see you," I stammered.

"You'll have to forgive Céilí for her anger. She is probably still scared," Feargal assured me.

"No, I'm not," she said.

"Yeah, why would she be? After all, she was the one who grabbed me!"

"Yes, I see. The problem is, Crooked Path can be very dangerous. There are a lot of muggings and she saw you hiding, so she thought you were a mugger. She's been mugged before. But ..." Feargal stopped and looked at Céilí. Céilí looked down for a second but then shot back, "We still don't know why the Yank is here. Maybe he *was* trying to mug me."

"The lad has a name. If I remember correctly, it is Orville."

"Yes, sir." I smiled, happy that he hadn't forgotten.

"I never forget the name of someone who saves me life. Now, Orville, why do ye come to visit us?" Feargal asked politely.

"Well, I came to give Céilí something." I gave a quick glance at Céilí, and saw her eyes widen, and then I reached into my backpack. I pulled out her shawl and handed it to her. Her mouth curled slightly, and I knew she was trying to fight a smile.

"You dropped this outside the restaurant today."

"And ye came all this way to give it back to her," Feargal jumped in.

"Yes, sir." I wiped my bloody nose with my coat sleeve.

Why?" Céilí asked softly.

"I really don't know. I guess, I just thought the shawl was so beautiful that it must have meant something to you."

"Now let's get ye cleaned up and have some tea by the fire." Feargal smiled.

"No, I better get back to the road to catch the bus."

"The bus goes to very late, and I'll escort ye down Crooked Path when the bus comes. Now teatime." Feargal clapped his hands and everyone scurried over to the fire except for Céilí. She had wrapped the shawl around her and stared at it for a couple of seconds and then up at me and said in a whisper, "Thank you."

An elderly Traveler woman handed me a piece of sheep's wool to put up my nose to stop the bleeding and a cup of tea to "warm the heart." I sat on a tree stump that was by the bonfire and nursed my tea as Feargal explained to the group of fifteen or so what had happened. There were ooh's and ah's as he retold how I saved him and laughs at my encounter with Céilí. A slight smile even appeared as I watched her across the campfire.

After Feargal told his story, he raised his tin mug and said, "Let us all give a toast to the lad who saved me life, Orville Jacques, and let him know if he ever needs the assistance of a Traveler, we will climb the Dublin mountains or swim the Shannon River to help our new friend."

The group roared and clanged mugs. The pain I had was quickly replaced with a smile of pride. After I told them all about myself, Feargal decided to introduce me to everyone individually. The ages of the people varied from a little boy of five to a woman in her eighties.

Everyone was kind, even the torch holder named Eamon who apologized profusely for scaring me. The last man in line I recognized. I knew I had seen him before, but I couldn't place him.

"Johnny, I want you to meet Orville."

The man smiled and put out his hand. "I think we have met before."

"Yes, but where?" I asked, puzzled.

"I was ringing me bike bell this afternoon at me old friend Seamus Flanagan."

"Yes, that's it." I snapped my fingers.

He turned to Feargal, "I gave Seamus a bad time for last night."

Feargal nodded, scratching his white beard.

"What happened last night?" I asked.

"I was in the pub playing me tin whistle when Seamus came in and said he was celebrating."

"What was he celebrating?" I asked, interested.

"He wouldn't say. But after a few drinks his tongue loosened, and he told the pub he had found one of the clues to the lost Mac Farlane treasure." Johnny chuckled.

"Treasure?" The word made my heart skip a beat.

"Yes. The lost Mac Farlane treasure is said to be worth millions and millions of pounds. But I think it's just a crazy old story." Johnny laughed.

Feargal interrupted, "I believe every word of the legend."

"Oh, Feargal, you believe in all those old myths." Johnny slapped him on the back.

"Myths? Treasure? Feargal, what's this all about?"

"I think we should get by the fire and have some more tea if you want to hear about the Mac Farlane treasure."

We all filled our cups and settled by the fire as Feargal took center stage with the flames as his backdrop.

"About a hundred fifty years before your man Columbus discovered America, there was a man named Mac Farlane. He was a sea captain and was considered the best of his kind—until it was found out he led a double life."

"What do you mean?" I asked.

"He was a captain of another sort. He was a leader of a secret group who paid homage to the ancient gods. A group of twenty of them were caught one night in an abandoned farmhouse, just as they were about to make a sacrifice. They were all taken to a jail house and, one by one, were killed in front of Mac Farlane, even his wife. The executioner was going to let Mac Farlane live another day, so he could spend the night thinking of what he witnessed and his upcoming death. But the executioner didn't know Mac Farlane knew how to pick locks.

When the sun came up the next morning, it revealed crows picking at the executioner's body which was lying in the courtyard."

"So what happened to Mac Farlane?"

"He got some of his other followers and took his ship and sailed in search of a new world. He left a letter saying that in the new world he would find riches beyond any person's belief. "

"And did he come back?"

"Some believe he came back forty years later, barely alive, with his treasure, but only his secret followers saw the treasure. He died shortly after his return, and they buried him with the treasure like an Egyptian king and drew up clues to his burial place."

"Why clues?"

"The clues were to different locations. Each location represented a different kind of danger. Ye see, to get to the treasure ye have to go through many fearsome obstacles first."

Not even the fire could stop the shiver that went up my spine.

"And Seamus, the house painter, says he found a clue." Johnny laughed and broke the eerie mood.

Feargal didn't join in. He spoke softly, "Seamus shouldn't spread rumors like that. The followers are still out there, and they might not take a liking to his drunken garble."

"What do you mean, they're still out there? How do you know?" I asked.

"They teach their children and their children teach

their children. They still meet in abandoned farmhouses and fields in the dead of night. How do I know? Sometimes one will die before the others can cover up their true identity."

"What do you mean?"

"The secret followers all have a branding of a snake on their right forearm."

"Why a snake?"

"The legend of St. Patrick was that he drove all the snakes out of Ireland. Having the branding on their arm is the followers' way of honoring the snakes and the old ways."

I gulped and Johnny laughed at the fear in my face. Feargal had me petrified.

"Enough of this idle talk, Feargal. Ye scared the poor lad to death. Let me take out me tin whistle and celebrate this lad saving you. He deserves a festival in his honor."

"Thank you, Johnny, but I really should head back. I promised my dad I wouldn't travel after dark and here I am."

"After that story, lad, you'll probably not break that rule again."

Johnny laughed and the group joined in.

"Well, Johnny is right. We should have a festival in your honor. Tomorrow night is our last night here before we head for Gleanndaloch for a week. Say you'll come."

I paused and looked at all the faces waiting for my answer and then saw Céilí's. Something made me want to know more about her. "Yes, I'll come by."

"Grand." Feargal smiled, "Now, I'll bring ye back to the road. Johnny, will ye come with us?"

Johnny smiled. "Feargal, your story didn't put a scare into yerself, did it?"

Feargal laughed and began walking up the path. The walk back was much more *enjoyable.* Feargal and Johnny waited with me for about ten minutes, laughing while rehashing how intoxicated Seamus was the night before. I didn't think it was funny and I finally spoke up as the bus pulled up. "It's too bad Seamus is an alcoholic."

"Who told ye that?" Feargal asked as the bus driver opened the door to let me in.

"He did. I'll see you tomorrow night," I said as I walked up the steps.

"He told you? Last night was the first time the man ever put a drink to his lips. That's what we thought was so funny. Why should he pick up a bad habit like that at his age," Johnny said, and Feargal nodded as the doors shut before I could say anything.

"And why would he lie to me," I said to myself . . .

I felt like I was going to drift off on the bus ride to Dublin. Thinking back on everything that had happened, it had been quite an adventurous day, and I was looking forward to getting some sleep. Of all the crazy things that had happened, there was one that troubled and occupied my mind—Why did Seamus get so upset when Johnny told him about his drunken behavior in the pub?

I could understand if he felt like a fool for being intoxicated, but that wouldn't account for the fear that shone in his eyes when Johnny broke the news. It also wouldn't account for his answer to me when I asked him what was wrong and he said he was an alcoholic. It made no sense. Unless he didn't want to tell me the real reason he was upset and made up a fast lie to quiet my curiosity. I didn't know, but I did know something wasn't right. I tried to put that out of my mind as an unwelcome thought invaded it—I wondered where Maria was. I grabbed my black stone and looked at it for a few seconds until I realized the bus driver was yelling, "Lad, Adalaide Road. Isn't this your stop?"

"Oh, yes, sir. Thank you." I put the stone back into my pocket and hurried down the aisle and off the bus. I was so used to the rain that I was surprised when the streetlights revealed how heavy it was falling. Just another fifty yards or so, I thought, and I'll be in Colm's cozy flat.

I thought I saw a figure standing on Colm's stoop, but I wasn't sure. The closer I got the more defined the figure became until I was about ten feet away. The light on the stoop lit him up, and I could see he was swinging a hammer slowly and methodically while laughing. It was Patch. We both moved at the same time. I turned so fast I almost lost my backpack as I sprinted through the rain. My soggy boots were sopping up water like a kitchen sponge, and my legs were getting heavy. I felt him gaining and I knew I had to find a public place or some people or else. The road seemed deserted. There must be a pub around here, my mind screamed, as I turned the corner and was met with an alley. I knew Dublin was his home court and an alley meant serious trouble. I grabbed trash cans and pulled them down behind me, hoping to slow his progress. It didn't. He seemed to pick up speed as I suddenly heard a tear and felt one of the straps of my backpack rip. I looked and saw the cause of the tear. It was Patch's hammer, which he was wielding freely, trying to strike flesh. I kept moving, trying to hold onto my backpack while looking ahead. Suddenly, at the end of the dark alleyway, I saw a neon-red sign. I knew it must've been for a pub, and I knew if I could get to that pub, I would be free. But the hammer felt like it was getting closer and closer as I could hear Patch's mumbled cursing. Out of the corner of my eye, I saw another trash can. I waited until he got close enough so he wouldn't have time to react and dodge it. At that point, I grabbed the can and pulled it down behind me. He cursed again as he wiped out and I picked up distance.

I kept my focus on the sign. I still couldn't make it out, but I was able to recognize the style. It was a pub sign. I was feeling a little relieved, knowing that even though he was gaining again, I would be in the pub before he could catch me. The sign came into focus, and I was right, it was a pub sign. There was something else we both saw at the same time, although our reactions were different. Mine was of horror; Patch's was one of laughter. It was the one thing separating me from freedom or death. It was a ten-foot chain link fence. I looked back and ducked away, just avoiding the hammer as it dug into the fence. Patch struggled to pull it free. There was no time to talk my way out of this one, so I took my backpack and swung upward, knocking him to the ground, where he lay panting and moaning.

I concentrated on each hole of the fence and surprised myself by climbing without any trouble and jumping to the ground. I got up and looked between the links and was face to face with Patch. He looked like he was going to try to climb the fence but then realized he now had no chance of catching me.

"I'm going to get you, Yank." He grabbed the fence and shook it furiously.

"Why?" I yelled back while heading toward the pub.

"Me brother Liam has to spend six months in the pen 'cause of you."

I ignored him and kept going until he hollered, "*My* watch says it's half past ten. Shouldn't ye be going home?"

Watch. The word stopped me in my tracks and I turned around. "I want my watch back!"

"Why don't ye come and get it!" He raised his fist, so I could see *my* watch.

I paused. I was tempted. The watch meant so much to me, but then I heard Will's voice inside me saying, "Don't play his game."

"Another time, Patch." I turned toward the pub.

"Yes, another time it will be," he said matter-of-factly. I knew he wasn't lying . . .

CHAPTER FOUR

AFTER THE DAY I had, I expected to sleep till noon, but a blaring police radio woke me up at 7:15. I rubbed my eyes to make sure I was reading the alarm clock correctly—7:15. I heard Colm on the phone shouting and then heard sirens in the distance. I jumped into my jeans and ran out into the hallway."

"Colm, what's going on?" I asked still half groggy.

"They found someone dead up the street," he answered as he hung up the phone.

"Dead!"

"Yes. I have to check it out." He put on his jacket and ran out the door.

I walked over to the window and opened the curtain and saw a crowd gathered in an alleyway across the street. They were all pointing. In two seconds I was out the front door and across the street, trying to force my-self through the crowd of onlookers. A policeman grabbed me as I tried to get Colm, who was hovering above the body.

"I know Colm O'Connell, can you let me through?"

"So does half of Dublin. That doesn't mean I'll let them through!" The policeman pushed me away.

"Colm! Colm!" I yelled, and Colm looked over and immediately nodded his head.

"Thanks, Donal, send him over," Colm shouted.

As I walked closer, Colm said, "Stay at least ten feet away. I don't want you to tamper with a murder scene."

"Murder?"

"Yes, murder. Now what do you want? I'm busy." Colm was agitated.

"I just wanted to . . ." I stopped and looked at the victim's face. I could barely make it out with all the smeared blood, but I knew exactly who it was.

"Oh, my God!" I gasped. "That's Seamus Flanagan!"

"How do ye know Seamus?" Colm asked.

"I met him in the alley off Grafton Street yesterday."

Colm turned to the other policeman, "See, I told ye that's where Seamus spends his time. He's always near Grafton Street. Why would he come around here?"

"And why would someone kill him in such a brutal way?" asked the other officer.

"They must have really hated him." Colm nodded.

"How do you know they hated him? And how was he killed?" I interrupted.

"It's easy to see they knew him and hated him because the only thing that meant anything to poor ol' Seamus was his gold tooth, and they knocked it out and threw it on the ground," the officer said.

"It's easy to figure out what the murder weapon was." Colm began, pointing at the forehead for the other officer, but I turned away.

"Yes, ye can see the hammer marks as clear as day."

"Hammer marks!" My mouth dropped to the street . . .

Colm forced me to leave the crime scene before I could tell him about Patch and his hammer. But, to tell you the truth, I wasn't sure if I should tell him, at least not yet. I was battling with confusion and sadness while I paced back and forth in Colm's flat. I was confused about Patch.

Why would he kill Seamus? I knew the motive wasn't robbery, considering I overheard one of the officers say that Seamus's wallet was still intact. I knew Patch had evil intentions, but would he kill for no reason? The sadness began to take control of my mind. I had met Seamus less than twenty-four hours before and now he was gone. I just couldn't seem to grasp the thought. I went over to the sink, got a glass of water, and then settled in Colm's sitting room.

Why would anyone kill a harmless man like Seamus, I thought over and over again. I thought of how Seamus was so kind when he carved the inscription on the donkey for my sister, Jackie.

I looked beside me and saw my backpack. I put the glass of water on the coffee table and picked up my pack and unzipped it. I slowly pulled out the donkey that Seamus had wrapped in an old cloth. I smiled sadly to myself, remembering him saying, "Now let me wrap the donkey for ye so it doesn't get wet." I took the old piece of cloth off the donkey and laid it on the coffee table beside my glass of water. I stared at the donkey for several minutes, admiring the craftsmanship, but most of all thinking that it had been carved less than twenty-four hours before. I couldn't believe, just like that, he was gone forever.

I shivered at the thought as I put the donkey on the coffee table. Maybe, I shivered too much because I knocked over the glass of water on the table. I used the old piece of cloth to wipe up the mess and went into the pantry and threw it into the trash. As I was about to walk back into the sitting room, I saw something from the corner of my eye. I glanced over at the piece of light-colored cloth and spotted that some parts of it were now black. I took the crumpled-up wet cloth out of the trash and unfolded it on the kitchen table. My eyes danced across the cloth as I recognized black lettering that was foreign to me. I knew what the lettering repre-sented, though; I had seen it on a few street signs and pubs. It was old Irish or Gaelic.

The words were spaced out on the cloth, and I tried to make sense of why they were there and why I hadn't seen them before. Then it occurred to me that the water must have made the dull ink legible. I raced into the other room and grabbed my Gaelic pocket dictionary, a pen, and notebook out of my backpack and ran back to the kitchen table.

I jotted the first word down in the notebook—líon and then looked in the dictionary in the L's until I found líon—full. I wrote it down and continued the procedure for the next five words until I had all the words.

My lips jumped as I read the translation out loud, *Full shine is key to kitchen.* "What does that mean?" I whispered. "What does that mean?"

As I looked at the cloth again, small red lettering appeared. I spent fifteen minutes trying to find the translation and decided to try to look it up in the names and numbers section of my dictionary. My eyes bulged as I found the translation for the red words—*Mac Farlane 1442.* I now knew the cause of Seamus's fear that day in the alleyway. I had the same fear. I had found one of the clues to the lost Mac Farlane treasure. Two words that I didn't have to translate frightened me the most—now what?

Everything was jumbled in my mind. I didn't know what to do or who to turn to. Should I show the cloth to Colm and tell him about Patch and the hammer? I knew if I did that, though, my chances of being part of the search for the truth would be over. I could live with that as long as I knew justice would be done. What I couldn't live with was the fact that if my dad found out about my adventure, I would definitely spend the rest of my trip sipping tea and eating soda bread in the Belltown Pub! Also, the only thing that connected Patch with Seamus was the hammer. It may have been two different hammers for all I knew. I didn't want to rush to any conclusions, but there was one thing I felt sure of—why Seamus was found dead near Colm's flat. He was coming to get the cloth from me. I thought back to what he had said, "Now, let me wrap this donkey for ye, so it doesn't get wet."

Wet? It was a woodcarving. It really didn't matter if it got wet or not. He knew he was in trouble for talking about the Mac Farlane treasure, so he wrapped the clue around the donkey. I gulped as I whispered to myself, "Did he break down and tell his killer he gave me the cloth?"

I needed a safe place to think. I checked my address book again because I knew I had cousins somewhere in Gleanndaloch.

" Perfect," I said. "The Travelers go there tomorrow."

I had a plan. I called my dad and left a message with the headmaster, telling him that I was going to spend the night in a bed and breakfast and then visit relatives in Gleanndaloch the next day. I had no intention of staying the night in a B and B. That wouldn't guarantee me safety, especially when I didn't know whom to fear. I left a lengthy thank-you note to Colm and then headed for the only place where I thought I'd be safe: the Travelers' camp . . .

It was early evening when I arrived at the camp. Johnny was the first person to greet me. His eyes told the story; they were not laughing. They were sad and swollen.

"Johnny, I'm ah ..." I stumbled looking for the right words but I realized there were no right words, "I'm sorry about Seamus."

"Thanks, lad." He forced a smile. "Seamus was one of me best chums. I feel partly responsible for how he went."

"That's ridiculous, Johnny. You can't beat up on yourself. Why would you feel responsible? You were at the camp."

"It's not where I was *at*. It was what I *said*. I thought Feargal was foolish believing those tales about the secret followers. I don't think it's fool's talk anymore." He shook his head.

"You don't?"

"No. I believe they were angry at Seamus for telling his tall tale and did him in." Johnny stared straight ahead in thought. "Maybe it wasn't a tall tale. Maybe he really did find a clue to the treasure," I said, looking to see Johnny's response.

"That's nonsense. Seamus was a part-time house painter and street peddler. How could he find a clue to one of the greatest treasures in all of Ireland?"

Feargal approached with the group of Travelers, interrupting our conversation. "Johnny, I know it's a sad day. But, me friend, put those thoughts away. It's time to dry our eyes and remember Seamus now that he lies ..."

Feargal paused, and I could see he was searching for a word to continue his rhyme.

Then he found it, "High above the moon. So, grab your whistle and spoons and honor his soul with a tune!" Feargal gave a warm smile.

Johnny brightened up as the crowd gathered around him and ushered him to the bonfire. He reached into his coat pocket and pulled out his tin whistle and raised it to the sky.

"This is for me chum, Seamus Flanagan. May this music make ye dance to the next world."

Johnny brought the tin whistle down and put it into his mouth and began playing. I was expecting him to play a sad song, but as he played, I realized it was an upbeat, even joyous song. I was so fixed on the concentration in his face that I didn't realize that Feargal had begun playing the spoons on his knee, and Eamon had picked up his fiddle and was strumming away. Suddenly, as I nodded to the rhythm of the music, I noticed that all the instruments that seemed to sound like they were going in different directions had joined as one, and it was a joyous jam session. Everyone was tapping their feet, even Céilí who was standing beside me. I looked over and smiled and she returned it softly. I had never heard this type of music before, but the way it built up and kept a steady warm pace brought this crazy feeling of happiness across my face as we stomped our feet and clapped to the beat.

It was almost as if the flames knew the beat as they danced behind Johnny, Feargal, Eamon, and a couple of other Travelers who were playing flutes and tambourines. After several minutes of steady jamming, Johnny stopped and the rest followed on key. He raised his whistle to the sky again, and we all yelled, "Hey!" Johnny smiled and everyone clapped.

"You'll rest easy now, Seamus Flanagan."

"Now, everyone, let's feast in honor of the departed soul of Seamus Flanagan!" an old Traveler woman yelled while stirring a pot.

I glanced around the group of Travelers and saw that Céilí was missing. Then, suddenly, I saw her walking in the distance toward a pond. Everyone was consoling Johnny, so they didn't notice me following Céilí. I followed her because I guess I was curious why she left the ceremony.

When I caught up to her, I stood behind her, a few feet away. I was about to let her know I was there when I spotted the charred remains of a house. Céilí was staring straight ahead at it, and then I heard her voice crack and she began to cry. I didn't know what to do. Should I try to comfort her? But then she would know I was spying on her. Before I could make up my mind, my foot snapped a branch and Céilí swung her head around.

"What do ye think ye are doing?" She yelled as she tried to hide her tears.

"I'm sorry. I . . . I . . ." I didn't know what to say.

"Spying on me, weren't ye?" She came toward me.

"Yes, I was. I'm sorry. I saw you leave the camp and I was just curious. Really, I'm sorry, Céilí."

I could see she didn't know how to react and after

a couple of seconds she finally said, "Well, at least you're an honest Yank." Then she turned her attention back to the remains of the house. I didn't say anything, I just joined in her staring. Everything was still and then I heard in the distance the most beautiful but sad sound. I guessed it was someone playing the bagpipes. I didn't want to ruin the moment by asking questions, but Céilí read my mind.

"Those are Uilleann Pipes."

"The sound is so beautiful. But it's confusing because it brings on a sad feeling."

"Indeed, it's a sad song."

"Who's playing the pipes? I mean, after Johnny's tribute to Seamus, everyone was so happy, won't this ..."

"Feargal is not playing the pipes in honor of Seamus," Céilí snapped and then realized she had, "I'm sorry. I didn't mean to . . . Do ye see that house that is barely standing?"

"Yes." I nodded.

"About seventeen years ago a couple moved into that house. Their names were Douglas and Mae Kemp. They didn't move there by choice. Ye see, Douglas was Protestant and Mae was Catholic. They were disowned by both their families and had to move out of Belfast. They thought they could escape the hate. It was here that they met Feargal and his wife. They all got along grand, because they were all great musicians, and since Feargal and his wife, Sinéad, were Travelers, they knew what it was like to be outsiders."

Céilí wrapped the shawl tightly around her.

"You say Feargal's wife. Wouldn't she be your mom?" I was confused.

"No, Feargal's not me da. He's like a da. So, now I come to why ye hear that beautiful sad song from those pipes. One night after the Kemps and the Travelers had music and dancing, the Kemps went home. A couple of hours later Feargal and Sinéad were awakened by the sounds of a blazing fire. It was coming from the Kemps' house." Céilí pointed. "Feargal and Sinéad both ran into the house and tried to save the Kemps, but only Feargal came out alive."

"Oh, my goodness!" I gasped.

"So, that is why he plays that song on his pipes, to honor the memories of his wife and the Kemps." Céilí was quiet and we listened to the song end.

"I like to think . . ." She paused.

"What?" I asked.

"I never talk this much," she stated.

"You can tell me. Really."

"Ye see there are three plover birds that come to the pond and sing. I like to think that is Sinéad and the Kemps singing like in the old days."

I smiled and Céilí took the smile the wrong way, "Ye think I'm silly, don't ye!"

"No, just the opposite. I lost a friend who lived by a beach, and I often think when I see two seagulls together on the beach, it is he with his long lost love. So now who do you think is silly?" I smiled and Céilí broke into a smile.

"I'm sorry, Orville. Feargal tells me I sometimes let

me temper get ahead of me thinking."

"I know that firsthand." I laughed, pointing at my eye that was still slightly bruised from our encounter. "Wait, you called me Orville and not Yank. Does that mean we're friends?" I put out my hand.

"Yes." She shook it.

I wasn't sure if I was about to make the right decision or not but I had to tell someone and I really felt I could trust her. "Then if we're friends, I have a secret to tell you and you can't tell anyone else."

"A secret. I love secrets."

"I've learned to fear them." I took a deep breath ...

CHAPTER
FIVE

THE NEXT MORNING I helped Céilí feed the horses before we left for Gleanndaloch. We didn't talk much. We
had done enough of that the night before. I had told her
everything about Patch, the hammer, and, of course, the
clue to Mac Farlane's treasure. Céilí could speak fluent
Gaelic and she confirmed my translation—Full shine is
key to kitchen—Mac Farlane 1442. What she couldn't
tell me was what it meant. We both had no clue. She did
tell me not to tell anyone else, even Feargal. Céilí thought
since Feargal was so spooked about the myth of the secret followers, there was no way he would let us search
for answers. There was no question in my mind when I
went to sleep that night in Feargal's wagon that Céilí
was going to be involved.

After we fed the horses and had some breakfast,

Feargal jumped up on his wagon and grabbed the reins. I followed and sat beside him.

"Orville, me friend, why don't ye go on Céilí's wagon. She could use the company," Feargal winked.

I nodded and jumped down. I was glad he suggested that Céilí and I ride together because that way we could discuss the clue more and brainstorm. I knew if I had jumped on her wagon on my own, Feargal definitely would have thought it was strange, considering Céilí and I didn't quite get along on our first couple of meetings.

Céilí had the same thought, "What do ye think ye are doing? We don't want Feargal to think we're chums."

"He told me to ride with you," I interrupted.

"Oh, aye." She moved over, so I had room to sit, and then flicked the reins and we were off. Feargal led the way across the meadow to a narrow, winding road.

"Orville, I didn't get a wink of sleep last night thinking 'bout all that treasure. What 'bout ye?" She kept her eyes focused on the two horses that were pulling her wagon.

"Yeah, me too. But it wasn't because of the treasure."

"What was it, then?" She gave me a curious look.

"It was Feargal."

"What 'bout me da?" she questioned.

"He shook the wagon with all that snoring." I laughed and Céilí joined in, "Yes, he sounds like a sheep with the bug."

We continued laughing for a while and then stopped suddenly, "If it's true and this is a clue to Mac Farlane's treasure, we might face some serious danger. If you want to forget about it, I'll understand."

"Stop right there." Céilí shot me a look that could kill. "I don't need yer protection, like yer Yank girlfriends."

"OK, OK. I just thought . . ."

"Ye thought ye would have all the treasure to yerself."

This statement made me fume, "Hey, listen. I couldn't care less about the treasure. I'm not in it for the treasure. I'm in it to find out who killed Seamus Flanagan, and I think this 'Full shine is key to the kitchen' thing might lead us to his killer. Don't you want to find the person who killed Seamus or are you just in it for the money?" I glared at her.

"Of course, I want to find his killer." She focused back on the road.

"OK, good. Also, Céilí, do you think I would have told you about the treasure clue if I couldn't trust you and if *I* wanted the treasure to myself?" I pressed. "So if I trust you, you better trust me or this won't work." I paused for a few seconds. "OK, enough of me Yank speech giving. Let's try to figure out what that clue means." I mimicked her accent and she couldn't help but smile.

"Well, Orville, I was thinking 'bout it all last night, and couldn't sleep. So I left my wagon and looked at the night, and I got a strange thought about the first part." She gripped the reins tightly as the horses worked overtime plodding up the narrow roads that lead to the Dublin mountains.

"You mean 'full shine?' That part?" I was intrigued.

"Yes, that part. I was looking at the big lovely sky and what did I see?"

"I don't know. What? "What?"

"A moon. A *full* moon. And it did *shine* all over the countryside." She smiled.

"Full shine. Full moon. Of course, I'm so stupid."

"No, 'cause I have no idea what the other part means."

"Yeah, what would a full moon have to do with a kitchen," I wondered out loud.

"That's the part that makes no sense." She nodded.

We didn't say anything for about an hour. We were both searching for a connection between a full moon and a kitchen. The farther we went up the mountain roads, the colder it got. Snow began to spit and a light fog formed. I spotted a tower peeking through the fog in the distance. I was going to ask Céilí about it when Feargal yelled back to us, "We'll stop there for teatime."

Twenty minutes later we had broken through the fog and were at the tower, which overlooked a grave-yard. I leaped to the soggy ground and checked it out. I knew instantly the graveyard was ancient because most of the tombstones were jutting out at different angles. There were a dozen or more sheep in and around the slate-gray stones.

"What is that tower?" I asked Feargal.

"That tower was built around A.D. 1100. It used to be a belfry. But when the Vikings invaded, it had a far better use. The monks would crowd into the tower and pull their ladders up in the doorway. That way the Vikings couldn't touch them."

"So was this a monastery?" I asked interested.

"Indeed, it was. Ye see, St. Kevin founded Gleanndaloch around the year A.D. 520. Of course, he was a very religious man. There are many legends about St. Kevin and how his monastery came about."

"What do you mean?"

"Many believe a young, beautiful girl named Kathleen drove him into solitude, first into a hollow tree and then to a small cave high up there in the sheer face of a cliff." He gestured to the bare face of the mountain.

"Why?" The story fascinated me.

"He became a hermit because he was respecting his love for God and fighting his love for Kathleen. Disciples came from everywhere because they felt that the sacrifice Kevin made to God was the greatest sacrifice of all—human love."

"Did these disciples ever see Kevin, since he was always high up in that cave thing?"

"They called that cave thing "Kevin's Bed." And yes, they did see him on occasion. Since he was so high up in the cave, there was never much food up there. So he would steal down at night and go into that building." Feargal pointed to the remains of an ancient dwelling that had no roof, and only the doorway and the walls were still standing.

"The holy men would leave him food in that building and that's how it got the name "Kevin's Kitchen.". All this talk 'bout food, let's get some ourselves. Johnny has some sausages on the fire." Feargal turned and was head-ing over to the flames. I was stunned. I almost couldn't speak but then I blurted, "Feargal, what's this called again?" I pointed to the ancient dwelling.

"Kevin's Kitchen."

"Did you say 'kitchen?'" I still couldn't believe it.

"Aye." He nodded.

"Is there ever a full moon up here?"

"Of course there is. Some people believe ye can still see St. Kevin up in the cave or praying in the grave-yard, but only when it's a full moon."

I knew it wasn't a coincidence. It was fate.

Feargal decided to make camp for the night about three miles away from Kevin's Kitchen. Céilí and I waited until everyone was asleep. Our plan was to pack our bags with stuff like ropes and flashlights that we thought would be useful for finding treasure. We would ride her horse, Gaby, together to Kevin's Kitchen. Once I heard Feargal snoring, I left the wagon and found Ceili, already mounted on Gaby.

The night was remarkably clear; a complete turn-around from the foggy morning. A light rain had fallen earlier, turning Gaby's path muddy as he lumbered on. A couple of times I almost fell off until Céilí said, "Orville, as much as ye may hate to, yer goin' ta have to put yer arms around me waist or you'll surely take a muddy bath."

I did as she suggested and then looked up at the

bright full moon and got lost in thought. Here I was, in the middle of the night, seated on a horse on a remote road in Ireland with a Traveler girl who I still didn't know if I liked, and searching for a treasure that was over five hundred years old. Either I was going to hear the director say, "Cut," my mother say, "Wake up. It's time to go to school," or this really was happening and I was crazy. What convinced me that I must be crazy was the fact that I really believed there was some truth to the clue, and we were going to find something. I just wasn't sure what it was.

"Well, there it is." Céilí brought me out of my trance.

"What?" I shook my head.

Céilí pointed to the tower up ahead.

"We're there already?"

"Ye been daydreaming for a couple of kilometers." She dismounted first.

"Yeah, I was just thinking," I said as I jumped down.

"Thinking we're both *mad*." She smiled.

"Crazy, was the word I was thinking of, but yeah, you're right," I laughed.

"There's only one way to find out." She tied Gaby to a tree.

Neither of us said a word as we got our supplies together. As we walked through the entrance of the cemetery, I turned on my flashlight. Before we could even think, we both jumped to the side, avoiding what was prancing down our path.

"What was that?" I tried using my flashlight to follow the figure, but it was already out of sight.

"A scared sheep. We scared her as much as she scared us."

"I guess so." I nodded.

"Now what?" Céilí asked as we edged further into the graveyard.

"Well, let's go over that clue again." I tried to sound calm but standing in a dark graveyard definitely made my spine tingle with fear.

"Full shine is key to kitchen," we both whispered and looked up at the moon at the same time. The moon was shining brightly above the tower.

"Do you think the treasure is hidden in the tower?" I asked while keeping my eyes on the full moon shining down.

"Full shine is the key, and the tower is the only thing lit up. So, it must be." She shrugged.

We didn't talk about what we had to do next. We both knew. I flashed the light on the entrance of the tower and entered cautiously as Céilí followed close behind. There was a bolted but modern-style door that separated us from the steps leading up to the top of the tower. Céilí looked at me for an explanation.

"Since that door is modern, they probably put that there to discourage break-ins."

"Well, there's no way we're goin' ta break it down. How are we goin' ta get up there?" Céilí frowned.

"It doesn't matter. I don't think we'd find any treasure up there anyway."

"How do ye know?"

"Well, the fact that there is a modern door means

many people have been in this tower. I would think someone would have stumbled onto a clue or treasure if there were any."

I turned my flashlight back to the entrance and began to walk out.

After a few seconds Céilí said, "Orville, come back in here." The urgency in her voice made me run.

"What is it?" I flashed my light at her.

"Turn your torch off," she demanded.

"Why?"

"Please, just do it." She waved her hand at me while staring above her.

I turned the flashlight off, expecting the entrance to become pitch black. It didn't. A thin beam of light shone through a hole in one side of the tower. It bounced off the floor and continued to shine through a small, round peephole beside us on the other side of the tower while continuing outside. It reminded me of the infrared beams that you would see in a movie about jewel thieves. Except this light wasn't laser red or artificial. This light came from the moon. We ran over to the peephole and peered through to see where the trail of light ended. We couldn't see the ending.

"How can the light be controlled like that?" Céilí asked as we scampered out of the tower and tried to find the continuation of the beam.

"I don't know. I have no idea. Maybe ..."

"There it is." Céilí pointed to the light and we both ran, tripping over gravestones, until we came to the ancient dwelling that had no roof, only walls and a doorway—Kevin's Kitchen. The light shone through the keyhole and reflected from one rock off the back wall.

"Full shine is key to kitchen. Of course, we should have checked this building first." I swore to myself.

"But we wouldn't have noticed the light."

"Yeah, you're right Céilí. It is very subtle. But since we followed it, we know there is more to that subtlety."

"Indeed. The treasure must be behind that rock!" Céilí sprinted over to the back wall.

"Wait, Céilí!" I yelled, trying to stop her. She wasn't listening. She crouched down and began tugging at the rock, trying to jiggle it loose. I saw it coming from a mile away. I didn't have time to think. I had to act quickly. I dove, knocking her to the side and inches away from the scimitar that came out of the wall and swung from side to side. Céilí didn't know why I knocked her over until we sat up, and the blade was a breath away from her nose.

"How did ye know?" she managed to ask after a few seconds of silence.

"Did you think that one of Mac Farlane's people would have his treasure buried without any traps?"

"I suppose not." She looked down.

Finally the scimitar came to a stop, and there was Gaelic writing on it.

"Céilí, look!" I yelled, trying to get her out of the daze she was in.

"What?" she was able to muster.

"What does it say on the blade?" I flashed my light on the foreign words on the scimitar.

"Oh my gosh, Orville."

"What?"

"It says . . ." She paused. "It says, 'If yer head isn't rolling in the kitchen, one final step in Gleanndaloch has to be taken. The hands may grab or they may give— Mac Farlane 1442.' Orville, this is terrible." Her green eyes were filled with fear.

"What does it …?" I stopped. "Céilí, do you see that?"

I pointed behind her to a row of four lights bobbing in the night.

Before I could ask, she blurted, "Bike lights!" and made a mad dash for Gaby. I followed her but was numbed for a moment when I heard the voice that came from behind one of those bobbing lights.

"So ye think if ye leave Dublin ye can escape me!"

It was Patch and his gang, and they were gaining. Céilí struggled with the knot she had tied on the branch of a tree.

"Orville, help!" she screamed, tugging at the rope.

I caught up to her, panting and wheezing. I pulled with her while watching the bobbing lights dancing closer.

"This way, mates!" Patch shouted.

Finally, the rope broke free. Céilí leaped up and grabbed my hand and I jumped up, almost falling, as Gaby, sensing danger, began his escape.

"C'mon mates. They're on the horse. Hurry!" Patch yelled behind him.

Céilí kept Gaby on the path that led us deeper into the graveyard. The bouncing bike lights were forcing us in that direction. At least, we were well ahead of them, I thought, as the lights fell farther behind.

"It's OK, mates," Patch yelled. "The Yank and the girl have nowhere to go!"

"He's right, Orville. This path leads to a deadend and then it's all steep mountainside. What'll we do?" Céilí's voice shook.

"I don't know. I don't know." I was trying to think of a plan when Gaby began to slow down and started whinnying.

"Gaby, c'mon, boy! C'mon me boy! Run!" Céilí begged.

There was no sane reason why Gaby stopped running until we spotted what Gaby saw. And to this day, there is no logical explanation. There, floating in the sky above us, was a man dressed in a monk's robe.

"This can't be real." My eyes froze on the figure that was gesturing us to follow him. Gaby had calmed down and without any direction from Céilí began following the figure down the trail that ended at a huge boulder. We could hear the distant voices of Patch and his gang, but it didn't faze us as we were mesmerized by the floating figure.

"What? What is it, Orville, a ghost?"

My eyes locked with the figure, and as crazy as this sounds, I knew who it was.

"Yes, Céilí. That's the ghost of St. Kevin."

He pointed to a place beside the boulder that looked like just a couple of bushes. We went behind the bushes and were on another path. He waved us on, and Gaby didn't hesitate as he ran harder and harder. I looked back and stared at St. Kevin. He nodded and then floated up high above the mountainside and disappeared into the sheer cliff face.

"Do ye think they found that hidden path?" Céilí asked after a few minutes.

"It would take a miracle to find that path." I put my hand into my jacket pocket and rubbed my black stone.

"We'll be safe." I paused, "For now ..."

CHAPTER
SIX

IT SEEMED LIKE we rode Gaby for hours down the hidden path until it finally connected with a main road. Céilí was familiar with the area and figured we were miles away from our campsite. There was no chance we would try riding to it, considering Patch and his gang probably had it staked out. What we needed was some sleep and time to think of what we were going to do.

It was around three or four in the morning when, after passing acres and acres of woods we saw a barren field with a rundown barn. Céilí didn't even have to direct Gaby, he was just as tired and knew this was the best place to stop. Céilí found an old pail and I pumped the handle of the well that was in front of the barn. After cranking it several times, water finally flowed out. Gaby drank first and deservedly so. After we had our fill, we brought Gaby into a stall and looked for a good place to rest. I don't know much about farms, but it was easy to see this barn was no longer in use. There were no animals, farming equipment, or even hay except for the bits and pieces up in the loft. We knew, however, it was our best place for comfort. After settling in the loft, we had a lot to talk about, and sleep wouldn't come until we cleared our heads.

"Céilí, I really don't know where to begin." I sat on the edge of the loft and swung my legs back and forth.

"Aye, I know. I guess what's troubling me most is that thing we saw. The ghost." She ran her hand up to her forehead.

"You mean St. Kevin."

"Orville, ye say that like it's an everyday thing to see the ghost of a saint."

"No, I think it's just as crazy as you do. But, I also think it's crazy that we found another clue to the treasure. And that there really *is* a treasure."

"So, what are ye saying, Orville?"

"I guess I'm saying we could talk about that ghost or whatever it was and try to make sense out of it, but we both know we're not going to make sense. We have no control over that. What we do know is Patch is real and his gang is following us, and they are good at it. So we have to figure out what we're going to do. Not to mention, the clue we found—the hands may grab or they may give." I stared at Céilí and she looked away.

"Céilí, you really freaked out when you read that. What does that mean?"

"Orville, it just can't be real."

"What?" I pressed.

"Any of it. Treasure clues, ghosts, and now this."

" Céilí, maybe we can make some sense of it if you told me." I was getting impatient.

"Well, ye know Feargal believes in all those legends."

"Yes." I nodded.

"When I was younger he told me about one that I think is connected to our clue."

I nodded for her to continue.

"Ye see, like most myths in Ireland this one has different versions depending on what county ye live in. And that's where the problem lies. What I'm going to tell ye could be just the work of a campfire storyteller, or it could be the truth. There's the Kerrigan's Keep version of the grabbing hands but ..." She thought out loud, "the clue said Gleanndaloch so it must be the Cain's Castle version. Yes, it has to be 'cause Cain's Castle is not that far away."

"OK, OK, just tell me, Céilí." I was getting anxious.

"All right, all right, I'm just saying like all legends this might have more than one version."

"I understand, go on with your version."

"Well, I don't know the exact year but back in the 1300s, there was this castle ruled by a man named James Cain. Cain was one of the most ruthless rulers around. He was a madman. He had no regard for anyone except for himself. He would use all the castle's money to build up his army, and then he would lead the soldiers to conquer other castles and steal from them in the most terrible ways. With all this wealth he acquired, he didn't help any of the peasants in his own castle. They would have small rations of root stew while he and his army would enjoy large feasts."

"What's root stew?" I interrupted.

"Exactly what it sounds like. Stew made out of tree roots."

"How sick." I shook my head.

"Indeed, very sick. He was a sick, twisted man. It got to the point that the peasants had enough. They planned an uprising. They were going to try to kill Cain. But, here's where the story goes strange. Cain addressed the peasants from the castle balcony. He told them that he had a dream that changed his life. In the dream he saw and felt the suffering of the peasants. So he felt with all the wealth he had acquired, he was going to change his ways. He was going to start by throwing a banquet in honor of all the good people of Cain's Castle."

Céilí waited for my reaction.

"That's really strange how a greedy man like that could change overnight."

"Well, that's what Patrick Mullen felt. He was the one who planned the rebellion. He told the peasants it must be a trick. But with all the excitement about being invited to a feast in the main banquet hall and broad-sides going up everywhere describing what it was going to be like, no one listened to him."

"How was it described?"

"Well, it talked about jugglers, tumblers, and fire-eaters. But, most of all, it talked 'bout all the food—pink salmon, spiced wild boar, and lamb all ye could eat. So they didn't listen to Patrick Mullen. Instead, they listened to their own hollow stomachs." Céilí sighed.

"What happened?" She had me on the edge of my seat.

"All the peasants entered the banquet hall. There must have been close to two hundred. There was only one peasant who didn't go and that was Patrick Mullen. The beginning of the night was just how the broadside described it. Everyone was eating and the faces that had gone so long without smiles were now laughing and enjoying the entertainment. James Cain sat at the head table sitting content, drinking his wine. He seemed like a changed man. Until . . ." Céilí looked down.

"What?"

"It could be the truth or just a story, but it still bothers me even if it did happen back in the 1300s."

"Céilí, please continue," I said softly.

"When it turned midnight, the atmosphere seemed to change. More and more of Cain's army entered the hall and stood by the exit. Unfortunately, the peasants had indulged in so many spirits and were enjoying the entertainment so much that they didn't pay attention to the soldiers as they slowly spread out through the room. Cain stood up from the main table and the room became silent as he raised his mug to make a toast. He said, 'I told ye good people of Cain's Castle that I had a dream the other night.' The crowd cheered, knowing that the dream was the only reason they were feasting. 'Yes, I told ye about the dream that changed my life.' The crowd roared again. What I didn't tell ye was about who else I saw in the dream.' The crowd stopped cheering and listened. 'Yes,' he began, laughing his demented laugh. 'I was waiting till I got ye all here. Ye see, in my dream I saw the old ones and they told me about a plot, a plot that my own people were going to murder me. The old ones told me to gather all me people in this hall and make them pay for not respecting me. With that, Cain clapped his hands and his soldiers pulled out their swords and clubs and began to kill every poor soul in the hall. Cain just sat on his throne, guarded by some of his men, and sipped wine until the last scream of death was let out."

"What a sicko!" I couldn't believe it.

"That's not even the worst part, Orville. Cain didn't even have the bodies buried. He left them in the banquet hall and had the door bolted."

"What happened then?" I shivered as I asked.

"Legend has it that Patrick Mullen went into hiding for twenty years and vowed he would avenge his people. The night finally came when he sneaked into Cain's chambers and abducted him."

"He didn't kill him?"

"No, he let them do it."

"Them?" I asked confused.

"The people in the hall. Or, should I say what they're known as, 'The Grabbing Hands of Gleanndaloch.' Patrick threw Cain into the hall and the hands did the rest."

"So what does all this have to do with us?"

"Feargal has showed me many times what he thinks

are the remains of Cain's Castle and the passageway down below ground to the banquet hall where it is believed the poor souls still roam. The clue says it all, Orville, the hands may grab or they may give. I used to think it was just talk, but maybe it's true. Maybe, because things have happened to the other people!" Céilí was jittery.

"What other people?"

"Well, the legend doesn't end there. People have tried going down there to find out if it was all just talk and they never returned except for the last one who tried it. Feargal said it was back in the 1920s. The man made his way back up the passageway covered in blood, screaming about the grabbing hands. The clue is leading us to Cain's Castle."

"I don't know if I believe in that stuff or not but after seeing that ghost tonight and finding the clue, I'm not going to discredit any legends. I want to find Seamus's killer and the treasure, but nothing is worth that type of risk."

I know, I know. I'm a wimp, but the story had me mortified and considering everything else, I was a believer. That's what scared me the most because we were dealing with the supernatural and being a detective, it's something very hard to swallow because it isn't logical.

After a few seconds Céilí said, "Well, that's your choice not to continue, Orville. But, I'm going to go to Cain's Castle tomorrow and find the truth."

"Céilí, just a little while ago you were saying all this stuff with ghosts can't be real. Now you believe and you don't care about the danger." I guess I was kind of upset that she had more guts than I had.

"Orville, I listened to ye. And I think yer right 'bout all this being more than coincidence. It's fate. And if I'm to die down there with the grabbing hands, then so be it."

Céilí tried to sound strong, but I knew she was scared. There was a force that was controlling her more than her fear. The same force was controlling me and I tried desperately to fight it because of my past experiences, but I couldn't. The force was curiosity.

"All right, I'll go with you. Now, you get some sleep and I'll keep watch." I smiled and shrugged.

"Watch?"

"Yeah, let's not forget Patch and his gang are still out there. They might be staking out the campsite, or they might figure we were smart enough not to go back." I yawned.

"Well, yer going to need sleep too, so wake me in 'bout an hour and I'll keep watch."

Céilí lay down on the bits and pieces of hay and in seconds was sound asleep. I sat on the edge of the loft thinking again how crazy my situation was. My eyelids were getting heavy, and I kept rubbing them to stay awake, but it had been so long since I last slept that need was taking over my mind. I'll just rest my eyes, I thought as I closed them for a second.

I don't know how long I was out. I was awakened by whispering coming from outside. I sat up quickly and went over to Céilí, who was still sound asleep. I put my hand over her mouth and shook her awake gently. She jumped a bit, but knew the look in my eyes meant danger and kept quiet. We were in the hayloft, and there was no time to get down and go into the stall for Gaby. The whispers became louder.

"Check the stall and see if the horse is in there," Patch told one of the guys.

We looked at each other, and we knew in no time we would have to do something.

"No, Patch. No sign of no horse," the kid answered.

Céilí and I stared at each other. We were baffled. Where could Gaby have gone?

"OK, OK," Patch answered back and then raised his voice, "So, not a bad idea to hide yer horse. But, ye got to do more than that to hide from me. Right, Paul?" he said to the kid.

We crouched behind a stack of broken boxes, and I peeked down below. The early morning light lit up Patch who was looking behind everything. I ducked back. I counted the different voices. There were four all together. I knew it was only a matter of time before one of them would climb the ladder leading to the hayloft. Finally, Patch said, "Hey, Davey, climb up there and see if they're hiding there."

There was nowhere to go. In a few seconds it would be time to react. Céilí grabbed my hand tightly as we waited, listening to each footstep up the ladder. The boy's head popped above and it was young Davey Evans. His eyes bulged when he saw us. I couldn't bring myself to hit him, he looked so scared. Instead, we froze, including Davey. Céilí let go of my hand and put her hands together quietly pleading with Davey not to say anything.

"Davey!" Patch yelled, "Are they up there?" Davey looked down at Patch and then back at us. It seemed forever.

"Well! What are ye looking at? Are they there?" Patch moved to the ladder.

"No, Patch. No, they ain't here." He blurted finally.

I wanted to sigh, but there was no way we could move.

"OK, Davey, then c'mon down!"

Davey headed down the ladder, and I peeked again and saw Patch pat Davey on the head.

"Why don't ye be a good lad and go outside and wait by the bikes for a minute."

Davey did as he was told, and I didn't like the sound in Patch's voice.

"Now what, Patch?" asked one of the others.

"Well, Adam, it's quite simple. We finally know where the Yank is headed. Cain's Castle."

"Ye mean that clue we read on the scimitar?"

"Exactly, Paul. All that talk in Dublin 'bout that bloke found dead and how he said he found a clue to the Mac Farlane treasure, well, when I was following the Yank, he met the bloke the day before he was done in. The guy gave him something. It must have been the clue that brought him to the graveyard in the middle of the night."

I had to give Patch a lot of credit. He was very smart. I wouldn't have been able to figure that all out if I were in his shoes. But, he wasn't smart enough. He thought we were already headed there, or at least I thought so.

"So Cain's Castle is our next stop?"

"Yeah. 'Cause the grabbing hands is from the Cain legend. Hey Paul, pass me that." I peeked again and Patch was pointing to a rusty can of paint thinner. Paul handed him the can and he poured the remaining liquid on the barn floor.

"What are ye doing Patch?" Paul asked. Patch ignored him.

"Adam, ye smoke don't ye?"

"Aye."

"Give me a light." Patch put out his hand.

"Why ye pouring paint thinner on the floor?" Adam hesitated and Patch pulled the lighter out of his hands and lit a piece of straw.

"That's exactly why I needed it." He threw the piece of straw on the ground and gave a look up to the hay-loft, and then the flames separated us. I heard him laugh as he ran out of the barn. The licking flames were devouring everything in sight, and Céilí started screaming at the top of her lungs.

"Calm down! We have to think of a way out of here!"

The flames were fighting their way up the ladder and the black smoke was blinding me as Céilí's screams stopped, and she went into shock. I grabbed her hand and pulled her over to the hay window and looked down. It was a fourteen-foot drop, but it was our best chance. I yelled at her. "C'mon, Céilí! We can do this!"

She seemed to be in a trance, "Me mum, me da," she kept saying over and over, while staring into the leaping flames.

"Céilí!" I shook her. "Your mom and dad want you

to live!" I don't know why I said that, but it brought her back into the moment. She nodded to let me know she was all right. "OK, on three!" I said and gripped her hand tightly.

"One, two, three!" We said in unison and jumped, landing hard on the ground. We lay there for a few moments.

"Are you OK?" I asked finally.

"Yes, I'm fine, thank ye." We both got up.

Gaby galloped out of the woods and headed toward us.

Céilí ran over and hugged him. "How did ye get out of yer stall?" She petted his soft mane.

"Yeah, I don't understand that," I managed to say, even though my heart was still jumping.

"He really is an angel," Céilí said as we mounted him.

"What do you mean?" I asked as we began riding.

"Gaby is short for Gabriel. Ye know, the angel who protects people from evil."

"Well, we sure could use Gabriel on our side." I grunted. What lay before us, I thought, could be worse. Much worse . . .

CHAPTER
SEVEN

CÉILÍ THOUGHT she knew a way to get to Cain's Castle that was off the main roads. She figured that not only would we be able to avoid Patch and his gang, but we'd get there faster. Time was now of the essence, considering Patch knew what we were searching for.

Part of me took in the beauty of the upcoming day. The sun was now rising and the morning was crisp. Gaby galloped along the sea of green fields, and we waved at the sheepherders as we cut through their land. It would have been easy to get caught up in the breathtaking atmosphere.

But then there was the other part of me. The part that knew danger lurked beyond those lush green fields. I thought a lot about Patch. Even though he didn't say anything to his friends, there was no question in my mind that he set that fire in the barn, fully knowing we were hiding up there. So, if that were the case, maybe he *did* kill Seamus. After all, three things pointed right to him: First, he had told his friends he had seen me with Seamus. Second, the night of Seamus's murder Patch was in that location. Third, a hammer was the murder weapon. Need I say more about that? But, something didn't seem right. Why would he murder Seamus? If he wanted information, why wouldn't he just rough him up? But, then I thought, he did burn down a barn. I realized there might not be any logic behind Patch McCormick and his motives. He might just be crazy and that's the worst kind of killer, because there is no pattern. You can't predict what he'll do next.

"Uh, oh." Céilí interrupted my train of thought.

"I don't like when people say, 'uh, oh.' What's wrong?" I asked.

"Oh, nothing, Orville." She tried to sound upbeat. I didn't buy it.

"C'mon, Céilí. Don't hold back. Tell me what's wrong." I asked in a sharp tone.

"Well, ye see." She paused as she pulled on Gaby's rope to make him stop. "We went a little out of the way."

"What do you mean a *little* out of the way?" I asked, waiting for it to come.

"I think we were supposed to go right 'bout two kilometers back." She said while directing Gaby to turn around.

"You know what that means?" I said frustrated. I knew Patch would easily get to Cain's Castle ahead of us.

"Well, I guess there's no use complaining about it. How much longer from this point?" I tried to stay calm.

"Gaby has had quite a night but I think he'll still be able to get us there in 'bout twenty minutes," she said to me and then put her hand on Gaby's mane and said, "Cmon, boy. Give me yer best."

We would be there in about twenty minutes but Patch would already be there, waiting. Then what?

We spotted the remains of Cain's Castle about two hundred yards away. The castle that was once known as a powerful giant now looked like an old man who had long been dead. Its skeletal remains were the only thing to suggest what a force it must have been—the bits of foundation covered the entire hill on which it stood. Gaby weaved in and out of the huge slate stones that were scattered in the courtyard. My adrenaline flowed the closer we got. Céilí didn't say anything. She just pointed about forty yards over to an opening in the ground which was in the center of the foundation. There were four bikes lying on the ground by the hole.

"What do we do? They already went down there." She whispered as Gaby brought us closer.

"I don't know. Hey, what's that writing on the rock?" I whispered back pointing at the red Gaelic words.

"It's a warning. Not to go down there because of the curse. I told ye, Orville, a lot of people take this legend talk seriously. What should we do?" She turned her head back to see my reaction.

I was trying to figure out a plan. I didn't care as much about the treasure as I cared about getting Seamus's killer—who must've been Patch. Even if he wasn't, he was an arsonist. As I was trying to form some plan, we heard a yell come from the hole.

"What was that?" We both said at the same time and jumped off Gaby.

The yelling got louder as little Davey Evans appeared up from the hole yelling and crying in a frenzy. He was holding a torch in his hand and was shaking it wildly.

"What's wrong, Davey?" I ran over to him.

"They're crazy!" He yelled at the top of his lungs.

"Who's crazy?" I asked and took the torch from him before he dropped it out of fright.

"Patch!" He gasped for breath, "Paul! And Adam! We all . . . went down there . . . but we got separated . . . and I think they're in trouble!"

"What do ye mean trouble?" Céilí tried shaking him for an answer.

"I don't know! I heard the most terrible screams! And I . . ."

Davey's face was white and his eyes had a faraway look. "Davey." I tried catching him with my free hand, but was too late. He fell to the ground.

"Is he . . . dead?" Céilí gulped.

I checked his pulse, "No, he just fainted from fright.

You better stay here with him until he comes to."

"Where are ye goin' to go?"

"Down there to find them." I couldn't believe I was saying those words.

"What are ye mad! Ye heard Davey!" Céilí's green eyes were full of fire.

"I know. But I gotta go." I grasped the torch and headed for the hole.

"Orville, let it be. We're over our heads with this. Ye might not be as lucky as Davey," Céilí pleaded.

"I'm in Ireland. How much more luck do I need?" I winked at her and turned for the hole. The joke and care-free attitude was strictly for Céilí's benefit. I was petri-fied as I began walking down the steps and through the countless cobwebs. After I walked down three flights of the twisting rock staircase, I looked above me. The en-trance of the hole was now just a little light dot. I must've been at least thirty feet underground. I gulped twice before following the steps down even farther. The deeper the steps took me, the harder it was to breathe. I breathed heavily and fast. I didn't hear anything. In fact, it was so silent it was loud. I know that makes no sense, but I kept thinking somewhere down here are three other people. Why don't I hear them? Something was wrong. The stairs finally stopped, and I was now level with the ground. I guided the torch along the walls and saw that there were three different corridors.

"Which one do I follow?" I asked myself as my teeth rattled. I decided on the middle one. I had no reason behind my choice. I knew if fate guided me this far it wasn't going to stop. As I walked down the middle corridor, I noticed the smell changed. It wasn't the musty smell that I had ignored. This smell I couldn't ignore. It was foul. I thought about turning back, but only briefly. Curiosity had me on a hook and I was biting. I continued on, waving my torch through cobwebs that had spiders as big as frogs. The smell got worse and I gagged a couple of times. There was a slight squeaking noise to my right, so I flashed the torch over to check it out. It was a rat as big as a cat. I yelled and it squeaked off into the wall. I was shaking uncontrollably, but I was trying to stay in control. "C'mon, Orville! It's just one little rat. It's just an animal. It's not going to hurt you," I said to myself. The fact of the matter is, I hate even little mice, never mind rats! I continued on though, turned the corner, and heard another squeak from behind me.

"Not another one!" I didn't bother to turn around. I decided to keep the torch in front of me.

The squeaks got louder and louder, but I listened to another noise that was right in front of me—a scream.

"Help! Help me!" I picked up my pace running into the darkness to the voice.

"Help! Help!" The yells got louder and I knew the voice.

It was Patch.

"Patch, I'm coming!" I yelled back and tried to ignore the other sounds but they were getting more powerful. The smell was, too. I kept stepping on something as I ran. I tried to ignore it, but I couldn't any more. I lowered my torch to the ground and saw an army of black eyes crawling everywhere. There must have been hundreds of them. They nipped at my boots as I screamed as loud as I could. It was like the rats knew my terror as they tripped over each other to get a closer look and take a nip at this unfamiliar flesh. I was ready to run back like a madman when I heard it again.

"Help! Please!"

I hesitated for a second but something forced me to go to Patch. I cursed the rats as I ran closer to the screams. Finally, I came to a door. What was beyond that door will haunt my soul forever. I opened it and there before me was Patch. He was sinking in a river of black muck. His eyes were filled with a combination of terror and bewilderment. He raised his hand up to me. I rushed over with my torch and waved it furiously. Then I could see what was behind the terror in his eyes. There were hands all around him. All different types of hands. Little and big, male and female, normal hands and skeleton hands that were covered with bits of ragged clothing.

"Help me!" He screamed and I grabbed his hand. I had it for a second, but he lost his grasp and, instead, I had grabbed a handful of air. I was about to grab again, when a strange urge came over me as I heard voices in my head. First, they were low. Then, they became louder and suddenly, I realized they weren't in my head after all.

"Let him go. Let him go. Let him go," they said over and over again. I felt the rage of power come over me. A feeling that wasn't me. I had control over Patch. I turned around and began heading out of the room.

The scream made me stop. I had to fight it. I sprinted over and waved the torch at the hands. More and more of them were coming up through the putrid, black muck and grabbing him.

"Let him go! Let him go!" The voices chanted.

"No!" I hollered and was finally able to grab Patch's hand and pull him up from certain death. We didn't even stop to breathe as we ran through the maze of bloated rats and up the twisted stairs, climbing two at a time until the small dot of light became larger and larger and finally swallowed us whole, and we were safe.

I thought I was going to pass out as I lay on the ground panting, trying to catch my breath. My heart felt like it was going to burst through my chest. I tried to focus on the faces around me, but they all seemed blurry. The voices were drowned out by the voices in my head that kept repeating "Let him go! Let him go! Let him go!"

"No!" I screamed.

"Orville! Snap out of it!" I heard a voice yell, and it was followed by a stinging pain in my face.

"Ow!" I tried shaking off the pain.

"Sorry, Orville. Ye were goin' into a state or something. I had to slap ye. I had to get ye awake," said the familiar voice. I was finally able to wash the other voices from my brain and find focus. It was Céilí. She crouched above me.

"Is Patch all right?" I asked.

"Yes, mate. I'm OK except for this awful pain in me leg," Patch answered while gripping his leg. Davey, Adam, and Paul ran over to him.

"We thought ye were a goner, Patch." Davey's face was still colorless.

"That's what I thought 'bout me mates." Patch gave them a faint smile and then winced in pain.

"Patch, I think ye broke it." Adam pointed to Patch's leg.

"Aye, I know. I want to go back to Dublin. The pain is awful. It's killing me!" Patch gritted his teeth.

"I said, 'How are ye?'" I looked from Patch back to Céilí and realized she had been talking to me.

"Oh, I'm OK. I'm just a little dazed."

"Well, ye really know how to put a scare into a lass," she said, smiling and pushed my hair out of my eyes softly with her hand. I returned her smile.

"So, did ye find any clue or treasure?" she whispered.

"That was the last thing on my mind," I admitted.

"What do you mean the last thing on yer mind?" she said a little louder.

"Hey, what I saw . . ." I began but was interrupted.

"Hey, mate!" Patch shouted.

"What?" I turned to him.

"I want to talk to ye."

"OK. Go ahead."

"Alone." He stared at Céilí and his friends. His friends got the hint but Céilí was hesitant.

"It's OK. Give us five minutes," I said to her. She

shrugged and followed the other three.

"All right, I'll talk, but you're going to have to answer a few questions first." I glared at him.

"I know what you're going to ask so just let me answer. No, I didn't kill the bloke in the alley. Yes, I did have a hammer. I found it right near the flat. It must've been the killer's." He grunted in pain.

"Then who is the killer?" I asked.

"That's what I wanted to tell ye. When I was down there being pulled down by ..." he stopped for a second, "ye saw it. I don't want to go into description."

I nodded. I understood. I didn't want to think about it either. "Well, one of the hands wasn't pulling. It gave me this." He pulled out a piece of cloth, and I got up and walked over to him and took it. It was the same type of material that was used in the first clue except the writing was in purple lettering.

"That's right! The hands may grab or they may *give*. They gave you the next clue, Patch."

"Yes, they did. But, that was before I was pushed into the grabbing hands."

"Pushed?" I was puzzled.

"Yes, I turned around and saw a shadow in the dark, and he pushed me. I'm telling ye it was probably the killer."

"Wait a second. How do you know? Considering what we saw down there, it could be anything." I was skeptical.

"I know. I know. But he talked and laughed. He was human."

"What do you mean?"

"He told me to give him the cloth, and he would help me. I said no, and he laughed a high-pitched laugh. He sounded like a Garda's whistle."

"Something seems strange here. Why didn't you just give him the clue? The treasure doesn't mean as much as your own life. Does it? And why are you telling me now, risking that I might want some of the treasure, if not all?" I wasn't going to give my trust away completely.

"I didn't give him the clue for the simple reason I had read it. Ye see, when I was staring at those hands pulling me down, I saw all the evil I have witnessed in me life. See this eye, me da give it to me. He used to abuse Liam and me. I guess I used it as an excuse."

"Yes." I nodded. I was interested but I was waiting for the relevance.

"Well, as those hands were dragging me down, I also saw the things I have done, including taking yer watch, and burning the barn. Ye knew I knew ye were hiding in the barn when I lit that straw." Patch paused for my response and I just nodded.

"Ye see, mate, in those minutes of facing death, I knew I didn't want to be like that no more." He laughed for a second. "I mean, I don't ever think I'll be in the St. Patrick's Cathedral Choir, but I don't want to live like how I was living. That's why I kept the clue and that's why ye have to have it. It's not 'bout treasure. It's bigger than that. It's bigger than all of us." His voice grew ominous.

"How do you know?"

"It says . . ." He took the cloth again and read it. "On the island of rocks rests a castle. Wait on the cliffs for the dark hours of the soul to find my grave. Filled with a treasure beyond any person's dream. Just one sip from the cup brings eternal life." Patch's one eye blinked.

"Oh, man. That sounds like an evil version of the Holy Grail!" I was blown away.

"I know and what do ye think will happen if the man with the high-pitched laugh finds it first?"

"You're right, I don't want to think about it. But, why didn't you tell your friends?" I was wary of Patch's turn around in behavior. After all, he chased me all over Ireland.

"They are all like me, but they didn't experience what I just did. I know it's hard for ye to believe me. But, show your lass the clue after we leave. Now get them back here before I lose me life from the pain." Patch handed me back the clue and I stuffed it into my coat pocket.

I was about to shout for them to come back when Patch said, "Ye could have left me to die, but ye came back. So here's your watch, Orville. It's a small enough repayment for my life. Why did ye save me knowing ye could die yerself? And, knowing I tried to burn ye down?"

"Because," I stared at him for a long time. "Because, I *didn't* want to."

CHAPTER
EIGHT

"Patch didn't tell ye where the island of rocks is?" Céilí said in between chewing on her sandwich.

It was around noon and we were finally eating in a little pub.

"No, he was so concerned about the meaning of the clue that I guess he forgot to tell me where it was," I said after taking a sip of soda.

"Well, it's the easiest clue of all. The island of rocks is the Aran Isles. They're covered with rocks. In fact, there are stone walls built all over them. Could ye pass the mustard?"

She pointed and I handed it to her.

"Why are there stone walls built all over? Are they there to separate land?" I asked, interested.

"Some are. But most were built because there were

so many rocks that settlers didn't know what to do with them. So they built walls." She looked at me plain faced and I laughed. Then she erupted into laughter.

"I know, Orville, it's mad, building walls for no reason except to get rid of rocks. But, they did this thousands of years ago on each island." She took another bite of her sandwich.

"There's more than one? How are we going to know which one to go to, Céilí?"

"That's where it gets really easy. On the cliffs of Inishmore lies the remains of Dun Aengus. It is one of the oldest remaining forts in all of Europe."

"Yeah, but it says castle on the clue not fort," I said.

"It was both. The unfortunate people used to mistake it as just a castle." She ran her finger across her neck.

"Wow. How do you know all this stuff?"

"Feargal taught me. He taught me almost everything 'bout Irish history, in fact . . ." She stopped.

"Go on." I leaned over.

"Nothing." She wiped her mouth and got up from the table and I knew not to push it, so I asked something else. "Speaking of Feargal, he's probably worried about you."

"Yeah, the same with yer da. Ye better ring him."

My dad, I thought, what can I tell him?

"If what Patch says is true, we can't go back to the camp. We have to go straight to Inishmore."

"Why? The killer thinks Patch has the clue," I said before I thought about it.

"Exactly, Patch is putting his neck on the line for us."

"He's using himself as a decoy to give us time. Céilí, I'll be right back. I have to make a couple of phone calls."

I called Colm O'Connell and reached him right as he was leaving to walk his beat. I didn't blame him for being angry at me. After all, I was rather brief and very vague with my information. All I told him was that Patch had a broken leg and to find him because Seamus's killer was looking for Patch. He must've said why a dozen times, and I felt kind of guilty for hanging up on him. But, there was no way I was going to go into detail. It was just too far-fetched to explain over the phone and hanging up on him showed the sense of urgency of the situation. Colm would have his men looking for Patch and that made me feel a little better about his safety. Then I dropped a coin and called Dad. He was in class. How lucky could I get, I thought, as I gave an excuse to the headmaster.

"Well, is Patch going to be all right?" Céilí asked as I came back to the table.

"I think so. Patch usually can avoid the police, but with that leg he's going to have to go to a hospital. So, hopefully, Colm can find him there before the mystery man with the high-pitched laugh finds him."

"What will Mr. O'Connell do with him?" Céilí asked.

"He'll put him in protective custody and grill him with questions, but at least the murderer won't get near him."

I paused for a minute. "Now, how do we get to the Aran Isles from here."

"Oh, well, first off ..." She stopped and looked in her wallet and then looked up at me and her face reddened.

"What's wrong," I asked.

"I only have two pounds to pay the bill."

"Don't worry about money, Céilí. I have enough to last us for a long time."

"But ..."

"Forget the buts, just give me the plan, and I'll take care of the money part."

"All right," she said finally, "I think first ye should give the barkeep a few extra pounds to make sure he watches Gaby until we come back this way. Ye see, we're going to have to leave him behind and take a bus to Galway." She finished up her soda.

"OK. How long does it take to get there?"

"At least four hours. Maybe even more."

"And from there we can get a passenger boat to Inishmore?" I asked.

"By the time we get there I don't think any of the ferries will still be going. But there are a lot of fishing boats that go over sometimes in the middle of the night, depending on if it's calm." Céilí yawned.

"You look really tired." I observed.

"Ye don't look so good yerself. We can sleep on the bus."

"Yeah, but we need more sleep than that. Also, I could use a shower. Do you know any place in Galway where we could get a couple of rooms for a few hours?"

"Well, there is only one place in Galway City that I know that rents rooms to Travelers," she said.

"Well, OK, we'll go there after we ask a few fishermen if its going to be a calm night. Now, let me go take care of the barkeep and ask him when the next bus is to Galway City."

When we jumped on the bus, Céilí let me have the window seat, so I could take in the scenery. I could try to describe the beauty of the landscape, but I don't remember any of it. You see, I was lost in the rolling green fields, my mind was filled with thoughts. I thought about the cup. If someone drank from it, could it really give one the power of eternal life? What if the mystery man were to find it first? I also thought about Patch and his transformation from evil to good. I knew what had happened to him was extraordinary, but could he change *that* dramatically? As my eyelids got heavier and outside my window became one dark green haze, it was then that I thought about what troubled me most—*me*. I played the scene over and over in my head. I could hear Patch's shrieks pleading with me for help. I could see myself ignoring it and walking away. Yes, I came back. But why did I start to walk away?

I didn't know. All I knew was I had to find the truth, and maybe then I would understand my behavior in that pit. The more I thought about it, the more troubled I became as my eyelids finally lost their fluttering game.

There were hands all over me, pressing against my face, pulling at my arms, and tearing at my legs. I couldn't see anything except bits of flesh hanging off the skeleton hands. Their droning voices were driving me insane, "You should have let him go. Now, it's your turn. Now, it's your turn." More and more hands covered me and all I could do was scream, "No!"

"Wake up, Orville! Wake up!"

I opened my eyes and realized Céilí and another passenger were shaking me.

"Are you OK?" They both asked, removing their hands.

"Yes, I'm OK, just a bad dream. Thank you," I said, embarrassed, knowing everyone in the bus was watching me.

The man nodded and went back to his seat.

"Orville, ye were in a dead sleep. I didn't think ye would wake up." Céilí handed me a handkerchief and I wiped the sweat from my face. She waited a couple of seconds while I caught my breath.

"What was the dream about, Orville?"

"It was about the grabbing hands." I handed back the handkerchief.

"What about them?"

"Just that they were grabbing me, but I really don't want to describe it." I cringed as I caught a flashback.

"Don't worry, it was just a bad dream."

"Was it?" I looked away.

"What do ye mean?"

"I mean, remember how you told me about the last

person who went down in that pit in the 1920s. He made it back but went crazy." I stopped while she nodded. "Céilí, I heard voices in my head. What if it's not a dream? What if I'm going crazy!" A few people looked back and Céilí gave them a fake smile to let them know everything was all right before she turned to me.

"Orville, it was just a bad dream. I have them all the time."

"What are you talking about?"

"Listen, remember when I told ye 'bout the couple who lived in that house that burned down, Douglas and Mae Kemp?"

"Yes."

"They were me ma and da. When Feargal and his wife Sinead ran into the house Feargal came out carrying me."

"That's why you went into shock when the barn was on fire!"

"Yes, it all came back to me. Like it does sometimes when I sleep. I was only a baby and Feargal says I shouldn't remember any of it. But I always have a dream and I don't know if it is real or not." Céilí stopped, but I had a strange feeling she wanted me to push her on.

"What is the dream about?"

She looked straight ahead as though she could see the dream in front of her. "I see meself lying in me crib wrapped in the shawl me mum made for me. It was this one that you returned to me. I see me parents slow dancing and and laughing. But, then I see flames and I feel like I'm going'ta burn up. I can hear meself crying and then I feel like I'm about to burn up. I see a man above me. I know it's not me da or Feargal. I can't make out his face, but he is laughing at me. He always laughs at me in the dream. Then I see nothing." Her face was pale as she looked back at me.

"That's terrible, I'm so sorry," I said.

"But, it can only be a dream, Orville. I was just an infant. What I was trying to tell ye was that after a terrible thing ye saw like those grabbing hands, yer going to have bad dreams."

"You're very smart for someone who hasn't gone to ..."

I felt like a complete jerk.

"School?" She finished the sentence and I nodded.

"After me parents died, I had no one to care for me since their families had disowned me parents for marrying out of their religion. So, Feargal raised me. He was there when no one else was. Ye see, Orville, ye know why I wanted to find the treasure so bad?"

"I don't know, why?"

"I want to go to formal schooling. I want to become a teacher. I want to teach people that the Travelers are not all bad people. We are all the same, but we are all different, too." Céilí's eyes danced. I knew she was excited, and I guessed she hadn't shared her dream with anyone else before. That made me feel really special as we escaped for the next hour from our bad dreams to our good dreams.

Galway City's cobblestone streets bustled with activity. We tried dodging the crowds, but Céilí and I kept getting separated. Finally, Céilí took my hand. I glanced over and smiled. Her wild long brown hair didn't seem to be intimidated by the gust of December wind. It almost welcomed it as her green eyes seemed to say something. I blushed and almost tripped over a street musician's open guitar case. We laughed, and then I threw a coin into the case to wipe away the guitar player's annoyed face. It worked. He brightend up, but we couldn't stop and see what he had to offer. The pier was just another forty feet. There were twelve fishing boats with nets draped from their sides.

Ceili began talking Gaelic to a fisherman. They talked for a couple of minutes.

"Well?" I asked when she was done.

"He said that there should be a few boats going over just before midnight."

"Midnight!" I repeated. The word triggered a memory.

"Yeah, midnight. Why?" She looked at me puzzled.

"I have it!"

"Have what, Orville?"

"Well, I've been thinking about the clue—on the island of rocks rests a castle. Wait on the cliffs for the dark hours of the soul to find my grave. We figured out the first part, but I kept thinking what the dark hours of the soul were and now I've got it."

"Well, what is it?"

"I don't remember if I read it, or heard it, but I remember the dark hours of the soul being from twelve to three."

"Do ye think it's a coincidence that the boats are going over during that time?"

"Céilí ,you should know by now, there are no such things as coincidences." I smiled on the outside. On the inside, well, that was another story.

We spent the next two hours shopping for supplies that we thought would be useful for Inishmore. I think our best purchase was a pair of binoculars that I bought from a street merchant. Right after he sold them to me, he packed up and got lost in the crowd.

We headed toward the place Céilí knew rented rooms. I wouldn't call it a bed and breakfast. More like a "You're lucky to have the bed, go find your own breakfast." There is no delicate way to describe it, except to say it was a rundown boardinghouse. In other words, it was a dump.

"Well, we're here." Céilí said with faked enthusiasm.

"Have you ever stayed here before?" I knocked on the door.

"No, never. But, it's the only place that puts up Travelers. I think they'll house anyone as long as they get their money."

"I couldn't imagine them turning anyone down," I said as the door opened.

"Yeah, what do ye want?" An apple-faced woman in her fifties peered out the door.

"Hi, we'd like a couple of rooms," I said politely.

"Money," she snapped.

"What?" We both asked.

"Money. Let's see it. I don't rent until I get me money." She put her dirty hand out.

"Oh, OK." I flipped through my wallet.

I could feel her eyes light up.

"Twenty pounds a room." The palm of her hand was almost in my face.

"Twenty pounds!" Céilí exclaimed.

"A room," the woman ordered.

"Ma'am, we're only staying for a few hours. We'll be leaving tonight around 11:30 or so. Could we make a deal?" I tried to be rational, but the woman didn't know the meaning of the word.

"Twenty pounds for each room. Take it or leave it." She started to shut the door.

"Céilí, let's just do it. I could use the comfort of a bed."

"OK, Orville, it's yer money, but she's ripping ye off."

Céilí shrugged.

"I know. I know." I handed the bills to the woman and she snatched them out of my hand.

"This way." She went into the house and we followed. She wore a tattered black dress. The sleeves covered her arms completely and the dress touched the floor. I imagined at one time it was probably very formal, but that was a *long* time ago.

"OK, ye take that one." She pointed to Céilí and then

to a room at the top of the stairs.

"OK, ye take that one." She pointed to me and then to a room beside the kitchen.

"Thank you," I said. "The woman gave no acknowledgment. She just headed back to the kitchen. I could see her pounce on her cup of tea. Céilí walked into her room and then said back to me, "If ye can believe it, it has an alarm clock. And it's not that bad looking, for sleep, I mean."

"Good. Set yours for eleven. And I'll set mine, too. We can't be certain enough."

"OK, sweet dreams, Orville."

"Yeah, sweet dreams, Céilí." I paused at her door for a second before retreating to my room.

I took off my coat and pulled out my black stone and looked at it. I thought about Maria briefly. Where was she? It was a strange feeling though as I thought about Maria, Céilí entered my mind. Was I over Maria? Did I like Céilí? I know. I was confused. I tried to analyze it, but I just got more confused. It was actually refreshing to think about something other than Mac Farlane's cup and his lost treasure. I woke up for a second, and I didn't know where I was. I looked over at the alarm clock—10:40. Why did I wake up? I asked myself. I didn't have a nightmare. Then I heard a voice from outside my door. It must've been the voice that woke me, I thought.

I put on my glasses and slowly eased out of bed

and headed for the door. I opened it just enough to peek outside my room and spotted the woman in the kitchen. She was talking a mile a minute on the phone.

"I'm telling ye one was a Traveler girl and one was a Yank. Yeah, yeah, yeah." She nodded and listened.

"OK, how far are ye?" she asked and waited for an answer.

"They said something 'bout sleeping for a few hours."

She waited.

"OK, I will. Yes, sir." She hung up the phone and looked my way, but I ducked back so she didn't see me. After a few seconds I checked again, and she was at the sink filling up the teakettle with water.

What am I going to do, I thought. Who was she talking to? We had to get out of here and quick. I hurried to get my stuff together and wake Céilí, but then I heard voices. I opened the door and Céilí was sitting at the kitchen table talking to the woman. Céilí spotted me sticking my head out the door.

"Orville, I see yer up. Come out here." Céilí smiled and I tried talking to her with my eyes.

"Is something wrong, Orville?"

"No." I said while trying to think of a way to tell her yes.

"Orville, Miss Jezzy has offered us some tea."

"Yes, call me Jezzy. The tea should be ready in a minute. I'm just waiting for it to boil. There's nothing worse than cold tea." Jezzy laughed. Her charm was a complete turnaround. If I hadn't heard the conversation,

I might have thought earlier she was just in a bad mood. But, I had heard.

"Thank you but we really should get going." I gave an emphatic nod to Céilí.

"No, please stay. I don't get many young visitors. I get very lonely. Please talk to me for a while." Jezzy practically shoved the tea down Céilí's throat.

"No, we really should go." I gave Céilí another look, and she knew from my tone there was trouble. She got up from the table and Jezzy put her hands up.

"Wait, wait! The tea's ready. I insist ye have a cup and tell me about yer travels." As she poured tea into each cup she kept rambling, "So, ye just came from Gleanndaloch. Was it snowing up in those mountains? That's about one of the only places in Ireland where the snow sticks to the ground."

"Wait." I held the cup and didn't take a sip.

"Wait?" Jezzy looked at me, fidgeting with her hands.

"How did you know we came from Gleanndaloch?" I stared right at her.

"The lass jest told me." She smiled over at Céilí.

"No, I didn't." Céilí looked back over at me.

"Yes, ye did. Ye said, 'We just had a long trip from Gleanndaloch.' Surely ye remember telling me." Jezzy tensed up.

"Orville, I know I didn't say that."

"Ye did!" Jezzy pounded on the table and hit my arm. My steaming tea went all over her and she let out a scream.

"Are you OK? Let me see your arm and we'll run it

under some cold water." I grabbed her right arm.

"No. No. No worries." She tried to shake loose, but I had a hunch and I was going for it.

"No, I insist. Let me roll up your sleeve and put your arm under some water." I faked sincerity and was able to get the sleeve halfway up her forearm. It wasn't much, but it was just enough to see it—the branding. The branding that Feargal had told me about—the snake.

"She's one of them!" Céilí screamed.

Jezzy threw a wild fist with her left hand and somehow connected with my head. My head rang for a second but I was able to push her to the floor and yell to Céilí, "Run!"

We grabbed our stuff and bolted out of the house, zigzagging up and down the cobblestone streets. We didn't know where to go, because now nowhere seemed safe ...

CHAPTER
NINE

We crouched behind the mountain of lobster traps piled on the dock, and I scanned each boat with the binoculars. After what had just happened, there was no way we were going to ask any of the fishermen for a lift to Inishmore. We couldn't afford trusting anyone for fear that they, too, could be a secret follower. We had to sneak aboard one of the vessels. Almost all of them had crews on the decks, checking the nets or sharpening their knives. It would be impossible to get past them unde-tected. But, then I spotted the last boat. No crew, just an old man standing on the bow holding a lantern in one hand. Every so often he'd look down at his watch and shake his head. The engine had a constant throb, and I wondered why the boat was still docked. The night mist had now become a steady rain, but it didn't seem to faze the old man as his mustard-colored raincoat absorbed the wet. He kept checking his watch and shaking his head. He must be waiting for someone, I thought.

His boat was our best bet, and I nudged Céilí and gave her the binoculars. She didn't say anything. She just nodded yes.

We crept past the other boats. The throbbing engine and the falling rain drowned out the sound of our footsteps as we climbed aboard the boat. The man was still perched on the bow of the boat. Céilí pointed below and I nodded. She headed down the steps, and I was about to follow when a flash of light blinded my eyes. I lunged on all fours to the deck and then slowly raised my head to see two lights coming from the dock—car headlights. I snapped my head around and searched for the old man. He was waving his lantern at the car. I crawled to the entrance that led below and then bounced to my feet and headed down the eight-foot stairwell.

"Psss!" I heard, coming from a couple of huge wooden barrels. I ducked behind them.

"I thought ye were right behind me. What happened?"

"Let's just say I think we have company. The old man was waiting for someone and they're here." As I finished the sentence, I felt the boat moving.

"Next stop, Inishmore," Céilí whispered.

"That's what we're assuming." I rolled my eyes. What if this guy was headed to England or someplace, I thought.

"How long does it take?" I realized I hadn't asked before.

"Probably between thirty and forty-five minutes. If that time goes by and we haven't stopped, we might have to let them know we're aboard."

I nodded. I didn't say anything because the rocking of the boat combined with the foul smell of what I guessed was fish guts in the big barrels didn't exactly make me feel talkative. I was feeling nauseous.

For about thirty minutes the only sound was the constant humming of the engine. Then we both heard a noise. Céilí stared around the left side of the barrels, and I stared around the right side. We saw black boots come down the stairs, one at a time, until a man was in full view. He wasn't the man we had seen earlier. This man was younger. His appearance made me shiver. His face looked like it had been raked with barbed wire. His eyes were black coals. It was like he felt eyes on him as he bobbed his head, pigeonlike, searching for an answer to his suspicions. Finally, he went over to a phone on the wall and picked it up. "Yeah, it's me. Did ye leave the light on down here?" he said as he turned his back to us and waited. "No. Ye sure . . . OK." He hung up and ran his hand through his salt-and-pepper hair. "Well, let's see. We're only a few minutes from Inishmore so ye might as well come out." He laughed.

At that point, I figured we should just give the man a couple of pounds for the boat ride, but then I felt Céilí grab my hand. Her look was one of complete fright.

"Come on out, will ye. I'm not going to hurt either one of ye." He moved closer to the barrels.

Either one of you, I thought, how did he know there

were two stowaways? He moved closer to the barrel. Now he was only about five feet away as he pulled out a knife. My heart was thumping and Céilí's eyes were bulging.

"Are ye coming out? Ye two are smart ones!" He kicked over the barrels and the fish guts flew everywhere.

Before I could do anything, the man had the knife to Céilí's neck and was dragging her up the stairs, laughing. My eyes searched for a weapon, but I couldn't find one. There was only one thing I could do—follow. I raced up the stairs and slid and fell on the rain-slicked deck. The man glared at me, his nostrils flaring as he tugged Céilí's hair.

"OK, Yank. I know ye have the last clue! Give it to me or I'll cut the girl's throat." He stopped and looked into Céilí's eyes for a second. "And feed her lovely green eyes to the sea."

"Don't give it to him!" Céilí screamed.

"Is it worth losing yer life over treasure?" He pulled her closer.

"Don't give it to him!" She screamed again.

"So, ye must've found out that there is more to the treasure than just gold nuggets."

"Yes, but how did you know?" I was trying to stall him as he edged closer to the side of the boat.

"Oh, I know everything about the legend and more. But, I don't have time to chat up with ye, Yank. Give me the clue, and I'll let her go."

"OK." I reached into my pocket for the cloth.

"Ow!" The man hollered as Céilí had bit him, and he dropped the knife. All three of us dove for the knife as it slid across the deck out of sight.

He grabbed Céilí again and picked her up. "I should've killed ye a long time ago." He didn't even hesitate as he threw her overboard.

All I heard was a splash and a distant yell in the night, "Orville, help!"

I finally spotted the knife and was about to reach for it when the man stepped on my hand. "Give me the clue!"

"OK, OK." As I reached back into my coat pocket with me free hand, I caught sight of a wooden fish club lying right next to me. He didn't see it. I continued reaching in my pocket, pretending I was getting the clue. "Here."

He reached down and in one quick motion I grabbed the club and whacked him across the face, and he fell to the deck. I threw the knife into the ocean, and then jumped to my feet. Céilí's in the ocean, I thought. I didn't know what to do. I could see he was recovering from the blow and was coming for me again. I ripped off my glasses and stuffed them into my coat pocket and dove overboard, plunging into the sea. When I surfaced, I hollered into the black night, " Céilí! Céilí! Céilí!"

There was no response. But, how could she hear me with the hammering rain and the booming thunder? Waves tumbled over me from all sides and salt water gushed into my mouth. I treaded water, trying to stay alive and trying to spot her at the same time. But, since the night was black, and I didn't have my glasses on, there was no chance of finding her.

"Céilí! Céilí! Céilí!" I yelled with all my energy. Maybe, too much. My limbs had gone from aching to almost no feeling at all. My vision was not just blurry due to my poor vision, but also my rain-stained tears. I had to make a decision. A white blinking light was about a hundred yards away. I knew it had to be a lighthouse. If I swam for the light now, I had a chance. The gripping pain in my legs and arms would keep my limbs moving. If I didn't swim for the light now, the numbness would continue until it overcame my whole body and I could no longer absorb it or move.

"Céilí! Céilí!" I punched the crashing waves and made the toughest decision in my life—I swam for the light.

I tried putting all thoughts out of my head and concentrated on the white light. It would blink on for five seconds, lighting up my path, and then it would blink off and the sea would go dark again. It may have only been a few seconds, but it felt like hours. It's hard enough swimming against the current under normal conditions, never mind the fact I was swimming in all my clothes and my hiking boots. I decided on a system. Every three blinking lights I would change my strokes from the crawl to the breaststroke.

As I struggled along, my mind began to wander. I thought of all the summers I spent taking swimming lessons at Cranberry Beach. I saw a picture of my parents with a picnic lunch. I smiled. I saw my dad slip a dollar bill to me, and me, a little boy, running across the blazing sand in pursuit of the ringing bell of the ice cream truck.

Two seagulls came out of nowhere and squawked in my face, jolting me back to the moment. I realized that I had stopped swimming. My mind tricked my body into giving up. The memory of Cranberry Beach, my parents, and the ice-cream vendor, I was going to take with me to the bottom of the ocean. That is, until the two seagulls woke me up. The seagulls hovered in front of me as I continued on, swimming the crawl. Each time my arms went into the water, I didn't think I'd be able to lift them out. But, somehow I did. An unexplainable force inside me was making me move. The blinking white light that was once a distant speck in the gloomy night was now bright as sunshine as my strokes became stronger and stronger, knowing I only had another thirty feet to go. The two seagulls looked back at me a couple of times to see if I was still following.

I rode the waves the last ten feet as the surf threw me onto the beach. I lay there coughing, spitting and thanking God I was alive. I staggered for a moment before I was able to rise and gain my balance. The memory I had been able to shut off for the hundred yards of frigid swimming came crashing down on me like the incoming surf—Céilí.

"Oh, my God!" I cried out on the deserted beach. I shivered and didn't know what to do. I had to get shelter and warm up or I too would die. My eyes were blinded by tears, so I didn't see the gigantic piece of driftwood.

I tripped over it and fell to the beach and swallowed some salty sand. I had to gain control of myself. I was falling apart. I prayed that my glasses were still in my pocket as I reached in. They were and so were my binoculars.

"OK, good." I mumbled to myself while trying to wipe my glasses dry. I knew that was impossible, considering I had nothing dry with me, but even with the wet smudges it was still better vision. I trembled uncontrollably from the biting air as I climbed up over rocks and onto a thinly paved road. Suddenly, I thought of the seagulls and stared back down at the beach. They were gone. There was no question they saved my life.

I stumbled along the road for about five minutes when I came to a house with a thatched roof. There was a light on inside and smoke was billowing from the chimney. I pressed my face against the front window, and there was a man working a poker in the fireplace. I inspected my hands that were a light shade of blue and could hear my quivering lips over the pummeling rain. I had to take a chance or else.

The man opened the door and my appearance must have said it all. He didn't ask any questions. Actually, he didn't even say a word. He just ushered me over to a rocking chair by the fireplace. He stoked the fire and it crackled to life. I was going to tell him what happened, but he wouldn't stop moving. He went and got some old clothes and pointed to the other room. I nodded and went in and changed into them and brought my wet clothes out and put them on the clothesline by the fire. I sat down in the rocking chair and noticed the man had put a wool blanket on it. I wrapped it around myself and savored the heat of the fire. The man came over, handed me a cup of piping hot thick liquid, and finally spoke. But, it was in a tongue foreign to me.

"What?" I said and then realized he was speaking Gaelic. "Oh, I'm sorry. I don't speak Gaelic."

"Ye don't?" He looked surprised.

"No, I'm American. But you speak English also."

"Surely, I do. But most of us choose our native tongue on the Isles."

I nodded and took a sip of the thick white liquid.

"Here's a spoon for yer chowder. Eat up."

I did what he told me, but I also tried to think of how to tell him what had happened.

"So, yer not a fisherman, are you?" He smiled and I observed his features. He was short, probably about five feet and he had lines all over his face. His hands were calloused and I knew he must've used them for work all his life.

"No, sir. I'm not a fisherman."

"That's what I thought ye were when I saw you."

"Why did you think that?"

"First, you looked half drowned. Second, I get fishermen all the time. You see, I live closest to the beach, and they're always falling out of their boats. The ones that make it back to shore always come back here to warm up. The ones who don't, come back the hard way."

"What do you mean *all* the time?"

"Once every few months. When I was a boy though,

it was every couple of weeks. That's why we wear these sweaters." He pointed to his white knit sweater that had a design on it. "See that symbol. That's my family's symbol. In case I washed up on shore and they couldn't identify me, they'd see this symbol that stands for Gill and they'd know I was a Gill. Thomas Gill." The man put out his hand, and at first I didn't acknowledge it because I was thinking of Céilí. How would she be found?

"Oh, ah, Orville. Orville Jacques."

"Nice to meet you, Orville. How'd you fall overboard?"

"I was getting a lift over from some fishermen when I went out on the deck and slipped and fell over. Then I swam for the lighthouse."

"Well, yer lucky ya fell when ya did."

"Huh?"

"The inlet by the lighthouse is always low tide this time of night. It's like clockwork. It may have seemed like a tough swim now, but if you had fallen overboard in two hours, the waves would have smashed ye against the cliffs or drowned ye in the caves. It almost happened to me when I was a lad." He threw another brick of peat on the fire and then got his coat.

"What was the name of the fishing boat?" He asked as he opened the door.

"I don't know. Why?"

"'Cause, they'd be worried sick 'bout you. So you warm up and I'll go to the harbor and let word out that ye OK."

"Oh, can't we wait till morning." I was nervous, I

knew once word was out, they'd be coming to look for the clue and me.

"That's madness. Those poor lads should know right away. You can stay in me guest room and sleep off your ordeal." Thomas Gill shut the door before I could stop him.

I looked at my watch and it was still running. It said 1:30. I had until three. That meant I had an hour and a half to find the treasure, or I'd have to wait till tomorrow night. I put on my coat and headed out the door. I knew I had to find the cup or at least die trying.

CHAPTER
TEN

THE RAIN BEAT down, turning my dry clothes wet. I followed the thinly paved road that ran parallel to the ocean and flashed my light at the beach briefly. The whipping wind and waves were flogging the shoreline. I was lucky to have survived, I thought, and shook my head in sadness at the thought of Céilí. Where was I going? I knew I was looking for the remains of Dun Aengus, which were on the Cliffs, but how do I get there? If I had a moon to guide me it would have been a little easier, I thought. But, the moon was hidden by the clouds and I had hardly any light.

I thought of the man with the barbed-wire face. Once he found out I was alive, I was no longer safe. I had to hurry. I picked up the pace jogging through the icy rain and powerful wind that cut through my clothes and rattled my bones. I cursed my poor vision, as I had to stop every couple of minutes and wipe my fogged-up glasses. Every time I thought the road might be heading up a hill to Dun Aengus, it would drop downhill. Where was it? I continued on hoping luck would lead me. Just when I was about to give up and go back the other way, I saw it. It was a sign written in Gaelic and English— Dun Aengus. There was an arrow pointing off the pavement to a dirt road. I followed the dirt road for about two minutes and then it ended. There was another sign. I flashed my light and read it out loud, "Dun Aengus trail ahead. Warning. No night access. Extremely treacherous. Great," I mumbled

There was a locked gate in between a boulder and a small hill. It wasn't that hard to scale, even considering the poor weather. After I hopped over, I flipped my flashlight back on and hiked uphill. I had to slow my pace down because there were all different sizes of granite rocks protruding from the muddy grass, making it slippery. I had trouble gaining traction. After about ten minutes of slipping and sliding, I made my way up the hill and spotted the remains of Dun Aengus. I read two signs. The first one said—*Danger Beware of High Cliffs*. I didn't have to be told that. I could hear the angry ocean in the distance warning me. The second sign was just an informational sign about Dun Aengus and when it was built. Now what? I had the clue memorized and went over it in my head as I shined the light on the remains of the fort.

"On the island of rocks rests a castle. Wait on the

cliffs for the dark hours of the soul to find my grave. Filled with a treasure beyond any person's dream. Just one sip from the cup brings eternal life." I whispered the words over and over as I walked cautiously around the rock structure. If it was like the other clues, there would be traps, so I had to be cautious.

"Wait on the cliffs for the dark hours of the soul to find my grave," I repeated as I took a deep breath and moved closer to the cliffs. The wind howled and I prayed that it wouldn't blow me over the side of the cliffs that dipped into the black ocean. I waited on the cliffs, staring down at the turbulent ocean for fifteen minutes. Nothing happened. Mac Farlane's burial place must be here somewhere, I thought. After all, the man was a sea captain, so this would be an ideal spot to be buried— overlooking the ocean. I waved the flashlight over the ground, checking for anything that looked like a burial ground. I couldn't find anything. There was just an area of rocks that stuck in the ground. No one could be buried there, I thought, and was about to continue on when something made me stop to think. I flashed the light again and noticed something. If I wasn't looking for it, I wouldn't have seen it. But, I *was* looking for it. The rocks formed a pattern—of a snake and an arrow. The arrow pointed to the right of the cliff to the ocean.

My wet skin trembled as I pulled out my binoculars and scanned the direction of the arrow. I knew the area I was looking at because there was a light that gleamed every five seconds—the lighthouse. "But that lighthouse was built hundreds of years later. He couldn't be buried in the lighthouse," I said out loud.

My mind was whirling. I knew Mac Farlane was buried somewhere in that direction but where? And why did I have to be up here during the dark hours of the soul from twelve to three? I could have found that clue anytime of the day.

Something Thomas Gill said entered my mind, and I raised the binoculars and peered into them again. With the dark night I couldn't see anything, but I didn't have to as I worked it out in my head—something Thomas said about the inlet near the lighthouse. I said his words out loud, so I could hear them clearly. "The inlet by the lighthouse is always low tide this time of night. It's like clockwork. It may have seemed like a tough swim now, but if you had fallen overboard in two hours, the waves would have smashed ye against the cliffs or drowned ye in the *caves!*"

"That's it! Of course, a sea captain would want to be with the sea. He must be buried in one of those caves!" I said. "I'd bet my life on it!" I shouted as I turned around quickly to go downhill and practically bumped into the figure.

"You lose the bet." He laughed. I saw his barbed-wire face for a split second. Then, I didn't see anything.

My scalp was pulsating and blood was spilling freely. For a moment I didn't know where I was until the high-pitched laugh rocked me. My body reacted, trying to move, but I couldn't. I stared down and realized the man had tied me up against one of the signposts. I grunted from the pain.

"Now ye know how I felt." He laughed and moved closer.

"Why did you tie me up? Why didn't you just throw me off the cliffs?"

"Because that would be too easy. I want ye and yer friend to suffer. Thanks to yer talking to yerself, I will have the cup that will give me eternal life."

"Wait. You said friend."

"Yes, tied on the other side of the post."

"Céilí!" I yelled over my shoulder to the sound of someone moaning in pain.

The high-pitched laugh rang in my ears. "I was hoping ye'd say that. No, the girl must be fish bait by now."

"Orville, it's me, Feargal," the voice said slowly, in pain.

"Feargal, how did you ..."

"Feargal is a well-respected Traveler, if there is such a thing. He knows many people. It was probably very easy for him to track ye. Right Feargal?"

Feargal cursed at him.

"Easy now, Feargal, me friend." The man went over and I heard the slap ring out.

"Ye see, Orville, Feargal doesn't like me too much. I guess it has something to do with the fact that I killed his wife."

He snickered.

"What? Who are you?" My blood was boiling.

"Oh, yes. Allow me to introduce meself. Me name is Eoin Mac Farlane." He put his hand out. "Oh, I guess ye can't shake it being tied up as ye are. I am of course related to Eoin Mac Farlane, the great sea captain. I have been searching for what's rightfully mine, and in ..." He paused and looked down at his watch. "In less than forty minutes I will have eternal life."

"So what do you mean you killed Feargal's wife?" I had to stall him.

"Well, about ..." He stopped. "Was it fifteen or sixteen or maybe even seventeen years ago. Which one was it, Feargal?" Feargal didn't say a word. I heard his moaning and I knew he was in pain.

"Well, anyway ..." Mac Farlane turned his attention back to me. "I was secretly doing my evil work when I stopped by this Traveler camp one night. There was singing and dancing and it made me sick. But what really made me sick though, was a married couple who was at the camp named Douglas and Mae Kemp." He cringed as he said the words.

"So?"

"So, don't ye get it? It went against everything I had been taught. I had to burn them. Feargal's wife was just an extra bonus! Ha! Ha! Ha! Ha!"

"You lunatic!" I tried lunging at him, but the rope held me back.

"Lunatic, madman, psychopath, whatever ye want to call me. They are all compliments. Now, I'll be back for ye and Feargal later. Feargal, ye'll probably be dead." He was about to leave. I had to keep him talking.

"Wait, what did any of this have to do with Seamus Flanagan?"

"The house painter? What a fool. He was painting a room in a castle near Dublin when he found the clue. I would never have suspected him until he opened his mouth in a pub and one of my followers told me."

"How many followers do you have?"

"I know what yer trying to do, but enough chat for one time. I will tell ye this. My followers are everywhere. But, we won't have to hide much longer and burning down houses will soon seem primitive." Eoin Mac Farlane turned and jogged a few yards and disappeared into the night.

I felt like I was going to lose consciousness when Feargal yelled at me.

"Orville, ye can't fall asleep or surely ye'll never wake up!"

"OK, OK," I said as I felt a sensation in my hands. The rope felt loose.

"I've got it!" Feargal yelled and the rope fell to the ground, and we were free.

"How did you do that?" I asked.

"I was working on it when Mac Farlane was on his tirade. I had to act like I was really in pain and weak, or he would have tightened that rope." Feargal stopped and looked at me long and hard. "Is it true about me girl, Céilí?"

"Feargal, I'm . . . I'm sorry." I hugged him and he began to sob, and then he sat on the ground and caught his breath.

"Lad, Mac Farlane is right. I am feeling death come on me. Ye have to try to get that cup before he does. I will just slow ye down."

"OK, I will."

"Now, there's plenty of rowboats on the beach by the inlet. Go, lad."

"OK." I headed back down the trail.

"Run, lad, run!" I heard Feargal yell above the angry weather.

I slid along the rocky countryside, splashing into the muddy puddles and leaping over the endless maze of stone walls. I was lucky Mac Farlane forgot to take my flashlight because without it my efforts would have been futile. With it, I had a slim chance, and that was all I was asking for. The pain from the blow to my head was now screaming throughout my body. But I wasn't going to listen to it. I couldn't afford to listen as I finally reached the road. I took off my fogged-up glasses and put them in my pocket. They were slowing me down, and I decided to put the flashlight in front of me and just keep running until I couldn't go on. I went up and down the roads, wheezing and coughing. I came to the last bend in the road that led to the beach. I checked my watch— 2:42 AM if my hunch was right, and high tide came at the end of the hours of the soul, I had eighteen minutes before the caves would be filled with water.

I spotted a fleet of rowboats on the shore and raced to one, pushing it into the tumbling waves. The numbing-cold ocean nipped at my legs. When I was far enough out, I jumped into the boat. I rowed in the direction of the lighthouse on the other side of the inlet. It was perched on some rocky cliffs, and I knew there were caves carved into those cliffs. I wondered how many caves there were, and in which one was the cup? My arms ached as the oars fought the changing tide. I was almost there, just another forty feet to the caves. I thought I saw something in front of me, and I stopped rowing for a minute and reached back into my pocket for my glasses. I put them on and spotted Mac Farlane in the same style rowboat about twenty feet ahead of me. He didn't see me at first because he was looking ahead at the mouths of four caves. I knew he was trying to figure out which cave was the one, and I heard him yell, "Yes!" and turn back and head for the third cave. When he turned back, his eyes almost popped out of his head seeing me gaining on him. But, then he smiled, a smile that was meant to intimidate me. I had gone through too much to let it faze me. I forced a smile, and then turned back and rowed even harder.

As I came to the entrance of the third cave, I searched for what he had seen and found it on the top of the cave. It was another rock design—a snake. I rowed as hard as I could as we both entered the mouth of the cave. It ended at a beach. He pulled his rowboat onto the sand and contemplated waiting for me, but then he looked at his watch. I looked at mine—2:53. In seven minutes or so, that beach in the cave would be filled with ocean water. He moved swiftly into the cave. I jumped out of the rowboat just before the shoreline and waded through the hip-high water. I had to catch him before he found the cup. But what was I going to do? I hadn't thought that far ahead and I reached into my pocket and rubbed my stone. Then I flicked on my flashlight and jogged, waving my light in front of me. I turned the corner and spotted Mac Farlane a few feet ahead of me. He saw it, and I saw it. There was a sealed coffin made out of rock with Gaelic writing on it. Secured to the coffin was the brass cup with a cover over it. It was within his reach. There was no way I would get to it before him.

"Wait!" I yelled desperately, trying to delay him as he removed the cup from the straps that secured it to the side of the coffin and then removed the lid.

"What?" He toyed with it in his hands, knowing my stalling was hopeless.

"If it's true about the cup, why didn't Mac Farlane drink from it? Instead his bones are in that rock coffin."

"Ye just don't understand, do ye?" He laughed. He was enjoying his power. I slowly reached into my pocket.

"His mission and promise were to die and rule from the next world. My mission deals with this world. Ye can stall all ye want, so the tide can rush in here and drown us, but when I drink from this cup, I can't be hurt from any ocean." As he brought the cup to his lips, I grasped my stone, wound up, and fired it at his brow. It struck him squarely in the head, and he dropped the cup and gray liquid poured out onto the sand. I lunged forward and jumped on him. He was caught off guard, and I was able to punch him in the face and stun him. I leaped up and grabbed the cup that still had some gray liquid in it.

I stared down at it, and the droning voices entered my head,

"Drink it. Drink it. He killed her. You will have power over him."

I was trying to shake the voices out of my head, but a force made me bring the cup closer to my lips.

"No! No! Don't, Orville! Don't drink it!" The voice shook the other voices out of my head.

I looked up from the cup and Céilí was running toward me.

"Watch out, Orville!" she yelled at the top of her lungs, and I turned and saw Eoin Mac Farlane lunging for me. I dodged him and he fell onto the rock coffin. I poured the last drops of the gray liquid into the water that was now up to my ankles. Céilí grabbed something from the water and then took my hand.

We waded as fast as we could go through the incoming surf as Eoin Mac Farlane followed hot on our trail. When we came to the mouth of the cave, there was a motorboat bouncing around in the surf. The driver shouted, "Hurry up! High tide is coming!"

We jumped onto the boat and I recognized the driver—Colm O'Connell.

"How did you . . ."

"I found Patch. I'll tell you later, we gotta get out of here before the boat gets smashed into the rocks." Colm revved the engine and was about to leave.

"Wait," I said, pointing to Eoin Mac Farlane, who stood at the mouth of the cave.

"Come on!" I yelled at him. A ride with us was his

only hope as the waves began to fill up the cave.

He gave his last chilling smile, turned around and headed back into the cave. In a few minutes he'd be joining another Mac Farlane in an eternal resting place— I could only guess where.

Thomas Gill invited everyone to warm up in his house as we sat around the peat fire. Céilí and I recounted everything that happened, and there were nods and shakes from everyone including Feargal, who gave a few disapproving looks at both of us as Thomas patched him up. I kept looking at Céilí in awe that she was alive.

"But, how did you make it ashore? I mean I'm from Cape Cod, I swim every day in the summer. But . . ."

"I found a huge piece of driftwood and held onto it and kicked my way to the shore. The strangest thing though, there were two seagulls that led me the whole way. I felt safe with them. I thought of what ye told me about how ye like to think about yer friend." She didn't continue because everyone else was watching. She didn't have to continue. I knew what she was talking about. I wondered if that was Will that guided us both to safety. I remembered what he told me—if I have any power in the next world, I will keep you safe. After everything unexplainable that happened, I felt that was the most concrete.

The next day I stood on the cliffs of Dun Aengus and stared out into the dark green ocean thinking about everything. I had been tempted by evil, and I almost caved in. But, I didn't. For that reason, I was grateful. Céilí approached me and she took my hand and smiled.

"Orville, I have something for ye." She handed me my black stone.

"How did you ...?"

"I had seen ye carrying it, and I knew it must've meant something to ye like how me shawl meant something to me. So, when ye threw it at that horrible man, I saw where it landed and picked it up."

"Thanks. I, ah ..." I looked into her deep green eyes and I knew it was right. She leaned closer and we kissed. We came from completely different backgrounds but we both had learned we were the same in many ways.

"Well," Céilí blushed, and I knew my face was probably the same color. "I better get ready for the festival. Colm is picking up Patch at the dock. It's a miracle the change that has come over that lad. It's a miracle."

I stared back off the cliffs and looked down at my black stone. Maria was right, I thought, the stone was filled with miracles and memories. She was also right that there would be a time when we knew it was OK to throw our stones back into the sea, so they would bring other people miracles and memories. I knew the time was now. I reached back and threw the stone as far as it could go until it disappeared into the sea. I heard the distant sound of a boat horn and it was familiar to me. It made me think of the *Island Princess* entering Belltown

Harbor, and I smiled. I remembered what my cabbie, Joe Ivory, had told me in Dublin, "You don't know where you're going if you don't know where you've been. "The boat horn called me. I knew where I had been and now I knew where I was going—home.

About the Author

T. M. Murphy lives in Falmouth, Massachusetts. When he is not writing or cheering for the Boston Red Sox, Mr. Murphy enjoys teaching creative writing to young people. He lives and teaches his Just Write It class in a converted garage he calls The Shack.